KU-083-848

"I'll add Casanova to the list – right after intimidating thug," Kate shot back.

"Let me start again," Jordan said quietly. "I trusted a woman I shouldn't have. But it was a mistake and I'm gutted by the impact on her family, which is why I haven't compounded their misery by publicly calling their mother a liar." He stepped closer. "Anything else?"

Kate struggled to return some sanity to the conversation. "You hardly *know* me."

"Not yet," Jordan admitted generously. "But I want to know you. And know you very well."

"You want to sleep with me you mean," she said to disconcert him. The man was insufferable.

His gaze swept her curves like a blue searchlight. "Hell, yes."

Available in April 2008 from Mills & Boon® Superromance

The Sister Switch
by Pamela Ford

Houseful of Strangers
by Linda Barrett

Her Sister's Child
by Cynthia Thomason

Mr Irresistible
by Karina Bliss

Mr Irresistible

KARINA BLISS

MILLS & BOON®
Pure reading pleasure

First published in Great Britain 2008
by Harlequin Mills & Boon Limited,
Eton House, 18-24 Paradise Road, Richmond, Surrey TW9 1SR

© Karina Bliss 2007

ISBN: 978 0 263 86155 6

38-0408

Harlequin Mills & Boon policy is to use papers that are natural, renewable and recyclable products and made from wood grown in sustainable forests. The logging and manufacturing processes conform to the legal environmental regulations of the country of origin.

Printed and bound in Spain
by Litografia Rosés S.A., Barcelona

Dear Reader,

The idea for this book came years ago when six couples, including Trevor and me, did a four-day canoeing trip on the same stretch of Whanganui River that Kate and Jordan navigate in these pages.

Blithely we set out, unaware of the physical and mental stamina required for the trip. And boy, did every woman end up squabbling with her man. The hardest part was in trusting your honey to steer you safely through the rapids, because we're not talking Jordan King here; we're talking complete novices.

What a great situation for conflict, I thought, listening to the relationship-testing arguments.

Trevor and I were the only ones who didn't have a fight, which confirmed for me that he was the One (convincing him took a year or two longer).

Karina Bliss

To Trevor,
The reason I believe in true love is you. And to
our son, Jordan, who I thought would really like to
have a hero named after him.

Acknowledgements

This book owes a lot to the support of Daphne
Clair and Robyn Donald of Kara Writing School;
Barbara and Peter Clendon and the readers of
Barbara's Books who encouraged me with the
Clendon Award; Kathy Ombler for her help with
Whanganui River research; my critique buddies,
the incomparable Writegals; and Romance Writers
of New Zealand and its founder, Jean Drew.

KARINA BLISS

figured she was meant to be a writer when at age
twelve when she began writing character sketches
of her class-mates. But a scary birthday milestone
had to pass before she understood that achieving
a childhood dream required more commitment
than "when I grow up I'm going to be." It took this
New Zealand journalist – a Golden Heart and
Clendon Award winner – five years of "seriously
writing" to get a book contract, a process she says
helped put childbirth into perspective.

She lives with her partner and their son north
of Auckland. Visit her on the web at www.
karinabliss.com.

CHAPTER ONE

SCANDAL.

The fashionable Auckland restaurant reeked of it, along with Chanel, the fruitiness of Chianti and mouthwatering stone-grilled meats so calorie-loaded Kate Brogan tried not to inhale too deeply. She was saving herself for the tiramisu.

Glancing at her watch, she saw that Lucy was late, as usual. Kate drained her water glass and caught the eye of the waiter hovering on the edge of the terraced courtyard, ostensibly enjoying the sunshine between duties, but plainly checking out his female patrons.

"Signorina?" Despite the fact that his taste clearly ran to full-breasted blondes, he was all politeness.

Kate smiled, her amusement growing as she watched him up her babe rating. "Antipasto for two and the dessert menu, please." Lucy might have the afternoon to play, but Kate had a deadline to meet.

While she waited, she scanned the place for diversion. This overpriced restaurant, its patrons a self-conscious mix of chic wives and corporate raiders, had always been a good hunting ground for her weekly newspaper column.

Across the courtyard a jacaranda daubed the diners in patches of sunshine and shade, while bright-eyed sparrows perched in its branches, quicker than the waiters to clear an empty table.

To her left an overripe politician devoured a much younger woman with his eyes, while his fat, moist hands stroked her upturned palms. Recognizing Kate, he froze.

She raised her glass to him, and Diggory scowled. Eighteen months earlier he'd lost his ministerial portfolio after investigations proved his taxpayer-funded business trips had doubled as dalliances with his personal assistant. Investigations sparked by one of Kate's newspaper columns, "More Bang(ing) for Your Tax Buck?"

To her surprise, he got up and came over. "You're back."

"And nothing's changed," she said dryly. "You can't be faithful to your mistress, let alone your wife."

"Margo left me," he retorted. "I can date whom I like. Since you've been overseas, I presume you missed my good news." He smiled, revealing smoker's teeth. "I was reelected last week." Kate sat back, stunned, and his smirk broadened. "Don't you want to congratulate me?"

"How did you rig that?"

Diggory's expression hardened but his tone remained pleasant. "A little breast-beating…public involvement with good causes…. People love a reformed sinner. I won by a landslide. What does that tell you?"

Her tone was equally pleasant. "That cockroaches have more lives than cats."

Diggory stopped smiling. "Now who's being a poor loser?" He leaned so close, she could smell the garlic on his breath. "It tells you, missy, that you don't get the last word."

"Your wife left you, didn't she?"

For a moment Kate saw violence in his eyes, then Diggory shrugged and stepped back. "I recommend the humble pie."

He left and, under the table, Kate unclenched her fists. Her hands trembled slightly and she frowned, not wanting to give him another victory. He'd still be sitting on the backbenches for the rest of his parliamentary career. But she drummed her fingers on her knees in frustration.

As she brooded, her gaze fell on a mismatched couple across the courtyard. The woman, whose iron-gray hair was cropped short, addressed her younger male companion in a manner as crisp as the white blouse under her navy power suit.

Jordan King. His size, looks and silky blond hair, which fell extravagantly past his very broad shoulders, would have distinguished him in any crowd. But in this conservative stronghold he looked like a peacock among pigeons. Sprawling on a chair that seemed too small to hold him, in his well-worn suede jacket and faded denim shirt, conspicuously in need of an iron.

His powerful fingers toyed with the delicate filigree ironwork of an adjacent chair, the softness of his hair at odds with his profile—all strong lines and clean angles. Despite the fair hair, his skin was tanned the translucent brown of wild honey.

By rights Jordan King should be gay.

The tabloids made it very plain he was not. He was also the only person in the history of Kate's influential column to turn down a personal profile. She could have accepted it if the tourism entrepreneur's refusal hadn't been so blunt. When she'd pressed, he'd said; "I wouldn't be comfortable doing the touchy-feely stuff."

Then he'd added insult to injury by asking her for a date.

"I wouldn't be comfortable doing the touchy-feely stuff," she'd retorted.

He'd laughed. "This is exactly why I don't give interviews…my comments are always taken out of context."

Six months later a bouquet of roses had arrived with Jordan's number and a note: "If you change your mind." As if.

Still, there was a slight smile on her lips when Jordan turned his head and recognized her. He smiled, too, eyes the blue of arctic ice sweeping over her, insolent in their frank appraisal. Kate frowned and crossed her arms, before realizing that only accentuated her cleavage under the open-necked green shirt.

His gaze lifted to meet hers and his message was direct, sexy and very explicit.

Hot color flooded her cheeks. He thought she'd been trying to pick him up, and his answer was definitely *yes*. She straightened and shot back a glacial look.

He shrugged, utterly arrogant, and turned back to his companion. The woman shook her head, said something.

Jordan responded with a wolfish grin, then glanced again at Kate, mouthing, *"Coward."* Adjusting his chair, he turned away and casually resumed his conversation.

Her mouth fell open. Picking up a linen napkin, she crumpled it tightly. No one should be so…so *raw.* There was no other word for it. He was blatant in his looks, in his invitation and in his dismissal.

"Get a haircut," she growled, and felt much better.

Tray in hand, her waiter approached, swerving sharply to avoid a collision with the slim brunette in a scarlet dress who was also intent on reaching the table.

Lucy sank into the chair opposite Kate. "Sorry I'm late." She peeled tendrils of long dark hair back from her overheated face. "She ordered for me, didn't she?" At the waiter's nod, she turned to Kate. "I was stuck in another postproduction meeting." A researcher for television news, Lucy often fed Kate leads the state broadcaster turned down as too hot.

"Don't worry, I filled in the time people watching." The waiter started unloading the tray and Kate reached for a sun-dried tomato. "Jordan King caught me staring and thought I was trying to pick him up."

"He's here? You're kidding me." Lucy swung around in her chair, then turned back, incredulous. "If I'd done what he's done, I'd go bush for a few weeks—or wherever he hides out when he's not empire building."

Obviously intrigued, the waiter busied himself with removing the extra cutlery.

"What did I miss?" Kate offered Lucy the focaccia, then took a slice herself. Jordan King built Triton Holdings from a small river-rafting company started with two university friends into a huge tourism conglomerate. Kate's boyfriend, Peter Walker, was contracted to develop accountancy software for Triton, but rarely mentioned King.

Lucy's silver bracelets jingled as she leaned forward, and Kate looked pointedly at the waiter, who had dropped any pretense of table clearing. He left reluctantly.

"He was caught in bed with a married woman…by her husband," Lucy said in a hushed voice. "Six months later, the couple is in the middle of a divorce and hubby has gone to the media, giving all the salacious details. He's bent on revenge, I'm guessing because he lost out on full custody."

The bread stuck in Kate's throat. She washed it down with a sip of water, aware of a strange disappointment. She didn't like King, after all. "Those poor kids," she said.

The two friends ate in a thoughtful silence.

"Wait a minute." Kate paused with an olive halfway to her mouth. "Isn't Jordan involved in setting up a holiday camp for children from broken homes?"

"Yes, that's what burns me up about it—the hypocrisy." Lucy brightened as she looked at Kate. "What a perfect topic for your column."

Kate ate the olive. "No," she said firmly. "I'm writing light and frivolous this week. No more crusades." And she avoided the subject of infidelity, because she didn't trust herself to be dispassionate about it.

"Oh, my God." Lucy clapped a hand over her mouth. "I just remembered we're here to celebrate your new independence. How was Australia? Did your baby sister settle in okay? More importantly, how do *you* feel?"

"Courtney loves the Townsville campus, and we found her some great roommates." Kate passed Lucy a dessert menu, and to her relief, her friend opened it. "And when I flew home on Sunday a postcard was waiting from Danny." She grinned. "I suspect my new sister-in-law is behind that thoughtfulness. They're having a wonderful honeymoon and—"

"I said how do *you* feel?" Lucy shut the menu.

Kate opened hers. "Great, absolutely fantastic."

Lucy reached across the table for her hand. "Sweetie, you've played mum to your brother and sister for years. Of course you're missing them."

To Kate's horror, she felt the prickle of tears. "I need to visit the bathroom. Order me the tiramisu, will you?"

In the ladies' room, she locked the cubicle door, leaned against it and cried— short, sharp sobs she tried to smother with toilet tissue. She was twenty-eight years old, for the first time in her life she had no dependents, and she hated it.

Hated not making dinner for three, hated not buying washing powder in bulk, hated finding the apartment still tidy when she came home from work. Last night, when she'd got stuck on the cryptic cross- word, she'd called out the clue… before remembering they'd gone.

She'd expected to be dancing for joy. Instead, she felt like she was missing her limbs.

Wiping her eyes with the damp tissue, Kate glanced at her watch. Ten minutes. She was taking too long. Blowing her nose, she washed her face at the basin and checked her appearance critically in the gilt-framed mirror.

Low heels, nondescript black pants, tailored shirt and a man's watch. Clean and tidy. Early responsibility had given her a pragmatic approach to clothes, though she always wore labels. They lasted longer.

She touched up her nude lipstick and dragged a comb through her short wavy hair, frowning at how red it looked under the lights. She was a brunette, damn it.

A button had popped open on her shirt; Kate did up two for good measure. Satisfied, she stepped into the corridor.

A door had been left open to the tiny utility courtyard, where crates of empty wine bottles were stacked alongside big bins. Leaves flew in on a gust of wind, and Kate went to close it. A shadow stretched across the doorway and she stopped.

Jordan King came into view, a cell phone pressed to his ear. "I'm sure if I lie low, stick with 'no comment,' it'll blow over…. Yes, Christian, I know how to lie low. Where am I?" He grinned. "Meg and I are having a quiet bite at Amici's." Jordan laughed and held the phone away for a moment. "Okay, okay, I'll make more of an effort. But no denials. I'm not compounding my error of screwing a married woman by lying about it."

Kate had heard enough. Returning to the table, she found Lucy stealing a spoonful of her dessert. Her friend's eyes widened when she saw Kate's expression. "It was only a mouthful," she said feebly.

"It's yours. I've lost my appetite."

"Listen, I was thinking…this is your opportunity to break out and have some fun." Lucy frowned at Kate's buttoned-up shirt. "I've got the afternoon off, you work flexible hours. Let's go buy you some sexy clothes."

Marking King's return to his table, Kate shook her head. "I've got a column to write." Women everywhere stopped talking to watch him. All Kate saw was a lowlife.

"Tonight then?"

She dragged her attention back to Lucy. "Pete's taking me out."

Lucy wrinkled her nose. "That wet blanket. Trade him in for a real man before he bores you to death."

Involuntarily, Kate's gaze returned to Jordan. Diggory walked past with his date, and for a moment the prince and the frog were both in view. She narrowed her eyes and pulled a notebook and pen out of her bag.

"In medieval times you could pay to have your sins forgiven," she wrote, holding up a finger at Lucy, who rolled her eyes and went back to eating Kate's tiramisu. "The practice was called indulgences—

possibly because you got to keep indulging your bad habits.

"These days the morally bankrupt buy a new image by making a hefty donation of time or money to charity."

She stopped and chewed on her pen, then scrawled the headline. "Do You Want Absolution with That?"

CHAPTER TWO

"Good God."

Kate grimaced at the shock on Peter's face as he stood at the door. She turned back to the hall mirror. "Too much?"

In deference to the formality of the occasion—a dinner dance given by Peter's software firm for clients—she'd reluctantly put on a skirt. Long, straight and black, its severity was offset by a halter-necked top of heavy white silk.

Looking at the expanse of bare skin and the generous cleavage the top revealed, she chewed her bottom lip. Lucy had insisted she borrow it. "I'm going to change."

"You can't, we'll be late. But…have you got a coat or something?"

Grabbing a crimson silk shawl from an

adjacent chair, she wrapped it firmly around her shoulders. "Remind me never to let Lucy loose on me again."

"I'm surprised she talked you into wearing something like that," Peter confessed as he watched her lock the front door. "It's not your style at all."

Though she agreed with him, Kate felt inexplicably piqued. "No, I'm far too ordinary for glamour."

"That's not what I meant." He opened the car door for her. "You rely on class, not cleavage. There's nothing worse than a woman flaunting her charms inappropriately. There's a time and place for that."

"On the weekend, in bed and with the lights out?" Kate regretted the joke as soon as the words left her mouth.

"Honey, I'm trying to give you a compliment here."

"Sorry," she said meekly, and got into the dark blue Volvo. Peter's conservatism had proved irresistible when his family had moved next door twelve years earlier, at a time when Kate needed respite from her father's disreputable private life.

When they were eighteen, she'd been the one who decided it was time to lose their virginity. Confident in his love, Kate had been curious to see what all the fuss was about.

Not much.

No, that was unfair. Sex proved very pleasant, occasionally even satisfying. But it had served to deepen her contempt for her father. To betray her mother for something as insignificant as *that*...

By the light of the dashboard, she looked affectionately at Peter's square profile. Close-cropped sandy hair—one shaver setting away from military—and a physique as solid as his character. As always, he was immaculately groomed, tonight in a black tuxedo. He threw her a sideways glance. "Tell me again why we have to wait?"

Kate sighed. "I thought we agreed to drop that subject for a few months."

"But it's far more sensible for us to get engaged now, and married as soon as possible." Peter had been doggedly proposing marriage for at least three years, and Kate's last excuse had just resettled in Australia. "We're throwing money away on two rents when we could invest in one mortgage."

"Oh, you mad, passionate fool, you," she teased. "And I thought you couldn't bear to live without me a minute longer."

"That goes without saying," he said briskly. They pulled up at the function center.

Kate hesitated. Being free of responsibilities felt empty right now, but she might never have the opportunity again. She had explained that to Peter and he'd understood—last week. Her door was swung open by a valet.

Thankful for the reprieve, she allowed herself to be helped out, then impulsively popped her head back in. "Tell you what, *I'll* ask *you,* when I'm ready."

Getting out, Peter handed the keys to the valet and strolled around the vehicle to join her. "If you leave it too long I'll run off with someone else," he warned, but he tucked her arm possessively under his.

"I'll bear that in mind." Kate kissed his cheek. "I won't keep you waiting long, I promise."

They started down the flower-decked hall leading to the function room. Peter stopped. "Listen, you know how I feel about Jordan King…. If by some remote chance he's here, instead of one of his partners, please stay out of his way."

Kate nodded, determined not to feel hurt. Peter had been anxious ever since he'd read her piece about his biggest client, despite her assurances that King couldn't possibly make the connection between columnist Kate Brogan and the guy overseeing Triton's software upgrade. Not for the first time she wished her boyfriend was more supportive of her work. He never understood the humor, and hated the adversarial approach she took when she got, as he called it, a bee in her bonnet.

She tried to categorize this failing like color blindness—not his fault. Plenty of people complimented her intellect; no one else offered her the emotional security Peter did.

They reached the doorway and paused for a moment arm in arm. It was an attractive room, long and narrow, the opposite wall more glass than plaster with its bank of French doors.

The panes were aglow in the light of the chandeliers, reflecting the bright colors of women's gowns, the snowy table linens dressed with gold bows, the glint of cutlery and crystal.

Kate squeezed Peter's arm. "I can tell it's your design, there's so much of the Midas touch."

She felt him relax, and realized he'd been scanning the room. "He's not here. His partner has come instead."

Kate accepted a glass of champagne

proffered on a silver tray, secretly just as relieved. "And I so wanted to pull Jordan's hair."

"Not funny, Kate," Peter growled. She was glad she hadn't told him she'd ignored three messages to call King. She wasn't interested in hearing his spin. Beside her, her escort stirred restlessly. "The thing is, I should really go and talk to the Triton guy."

"Go ahead. I understand why you're not keen to introduce us." She waved to a group of women by the bar. "I'll get in some practice and join the other neglected wives."

"You're wonderful," said Peter, and was gone.

Kate watched his retreating back, knowing she wouldn't see him until dinner, and then only briefly. He was an ambitious and tireless worker. Yet another point of difference from her father, who had flitted from one crazy scheme to another.

Exchanging pleasantries with the other women, Kate eyed Peter's target with some surprise. Jordan King's partner, also gorgeous, was urbanity personified, as suave and dark as King was brash and blond.

As she wondered idly whether he was as tall, the comparison became unnervingly easy. Jordan King, his arm around the waist of a stunning blonde, appeared beside him. His horror almost comical, Peter sought Kate's gaze. Abruptly, she turned away, startling one of the women, who had been detailing her child's case of chicken pox. "It's not *that* contagious," she insisted.

Kate forced herself to turn around again. "I'm sorry." She searched for an excuse but found none. "Actually, there's someone over there I don't want to meet," she confessed, then could have kicked herself as four pairs of eyes swept the room.

"Male or female?"

"Female," lied Kate. She knew King's attention had settled on the group, drawn by the frisson of excitement, and she kept her face averted. It wasn't in her nature to avoid a confrontation, but she had to do this for Peter.

"What a honey that one is," said the sales manager's wife, sending a come-talk-to-us invitation.

Kate gave up. "Excuse me." Bolting for the powder room, she reflected that if she wanted to remain undetected she'd have to stay away from Peter, plus stick to the company of men, who'd be unaffected by Jordan's sex appeal.

JORDAN WATCHED HER GO.

Run, Kate Brogan! But I have you in my sights.

It had been so easy picking her out of the crowd. Peter Walker had betrayed her location with one glance. The guy was as good as a heat-seeking missile.

"How the hell did you persuade Jordan to escort you to such a civilized gathering, Monique? I didn't know a sister carried that sort of clout."

Jordan turned back to his partner. They'd been friends too long for Christian to really be startled by anything he did.

"Believe it or not, he asked me to come." She turned to Peter, holding out her hand. "We haven't met. I'm Monique King, and it appears we're gate-crashers."

Though obviously dismayed, Peter managed to say all the right things, Jordan noted with wry amusement.

Until Triton's software developer had tapped on Jordan's door that afternoon, their previous acquaintance had been limited to quarterly updates. Christian, who handled the company's acquisitions, and Luke, before he'd spearheaded their new charitable trust, worked more closely with their contractor. Jordan's restless vitality better suited him to operational concerns.

Fuming because Kate Brogan wasn't returning his calls, Jordan hadn't been in the mood for a quiet word with the project manager, but by the end of the man's speech he'd been riveted.

Peter would "hate it if Jordan discovered his relationship with Kate from someone else." He wanted to "reassure" Jordan that none of Kate's information for her column had come from him. Peter would never be that "disloyal."

Jordan had assured him that he was now fully aware of Peter's capacity for loyalty.

"Champagne?" Accepting the glass Peter offered, Jordan returned the man's toast, and wondered what the hell Kate saw in him. Not that he could criticize, given his own recent poor judgment.

Though he was as angry with Penny as her cuckolded husband, Jordan saw no honor in petty revenge. So when the scandal broke, he'd kept his mouth shut and hunkered down to weather it.

That's why he'd declined Kate's request for a profile. Plus, he'd promised his partners to stop talking to the press altogether.

They still remembered the time a sense of mischief had prompted him to tell one pompous business reporter that Triton was thinking about diversifying its portfolio into raising grasshoppers for the pet market.

The scoop had gone to print, and the temporary drop in Triton's share price had convinced Luke and Christian that their partner's black humor was best shared only with those who knew him well.

The same sense of mischief had made Jordan ask Kate out after refusing her interview. He knew he'd pricked her professional ego by his refusal, knew she hated finding out she had one.

Her response had intrigued him enough to start reading her column.

Jordan lifted his glass. "To an interesting evening." He laughed when Christian narrowed his eyes.

BY KEEPING A CAREFUL distance, Kate found the evening passed quite pleasantly. After dinner, she even discovered a quiet corner to sit alone with a coffee and jot down a few ideas, grateful for the respite from networking.

A shadow fell over the table and, intent on her work, she put a hand over her cup. "No more coffee, thanks."

"Actually, I wanted to ask you to dance." The voice was deep, powerful, definitely not that of her waitress. Kate looked up to see Jordan King regarding her with such a charming smile, she immediately felt like Little Red Riding Hood.

"At least," he said approvingly, "you're not going to feign surprise at seeing me."

She looked pointedly at his long hair, lying loose around his shoulders, and the gold hoop in his left ear. Tonight, the shirt was ironed, but the fineness of the cream silk gave it a transparency that was almost indecent. He wore camel-colored pants and well-worn boots in a room where every other man wore a suit. "I think everyone's seen you."

He threw back his head and laughed, a

deep, melodious sound that turned heads. "About that dance…"

Remembering her promise to Peter, Kate said nicely, "Don't tell me your dance card's empty. I won't believe it."

"I had a cancellation."

"Then a little rest will do you good."

"I'd love to join you, of course…" he paused to enjoy her alarm "…but I have commitments elsewhere."

Kate lifted her chin. "Let's talk about the column in business hours, Jordan. I don't want any civilians caught in the cross fire." She resisted the urge to check where Peter was.

"I tried that," he said. "You wouldn't return my calls. But contrary to what you think, I can behave myself when I have to."

Because she doubted that, Kate tested him. "You really want to dance with someone who called you Tarzan in a business suit?"

"The reference to the business suit was libelous," Jordan said. "I don't own one."

He held out a hand. "One dance, Kate, then I'll go away."

Reluctantly, she put her hand in his, felt his grasp like a brand and pulled away.

"Sparks." Jordan reclaimed her hand and tucked it firmly under his forearm. "Next you'll be accusing me of betraying my eco convictions by wearing nylon underwear."

Kate bit her lip. She would *not* be amused.

"I don't think you'll be needing this, do you?" He removed her protective crimson shawl as carelessly as a child unwrapping a birthday present, and dropped it on an empty chair. "It's so hot in here."

Kate narrowed her eyes, but his expression was guileless. She turned toward the dance floor and her steps faltered. With the evening drawing to a close, couples were enjoying the intimacy of the low lighting and the slow, sensual beat of the music.

Swinging around to face Jordan, she held her arms out stiffly, determined to keep some distance between them. She caught the amusement in his eyes as he stepped forward, gesturing toward the bar, where Peter sat in animated conversation with a colleague. "Your boyfriend, I believe?"

Kate hesitated. "Yes."

"Pity."

She blushed. "Is that some sort of compliment?"

"No, pity. He seems like a nice guy."

Choking back a laugh, Kate looked up at Jordan, then wished she hadn't. She could see eternal possibilities in those eyes.

"But I still have to take you away from him," he said. She stumbled and he drew her closer, his arm dropping to encircle her waist.

"*What* did you say?"

"I have to take you away from him." He stared at her. "For the dance."

Feeling foolish, she shifted her gaze. "He'll probably be grateful. He hates to dance."

"But you love it, especially on the moral high ground."

It would take better bait than that to get a rise out of her.

"Don't marry Peter. You don't suit."

Kate stopped dead. "You're very opinionated, for someone who barely knows me."

"Funny, I was going to say the same thing about you. Writing about me in your column." He moved his hand soothingly on her bare back, and she found herself dancing again, somehow closer than before.

"'By their deeds ye shall know them,'" she quoted softly. "My column looks at social inconsistencies, including the differences between what people say and what they do." As a columnist satirizing human foibles and failings, she had grown accustomed to the disgruntled seeking their revenge. And she knew how to handle them.

"You're leading, Kate."

She stumbled and bit back an automatic

apology. No apologies tonight, not to this man. "It's the legacy of learning to dance at an all-girls' school."

"Yeah, I had you pegged as a convent girl."

Kate quelled another pang of annoyance. "Let's get back on topic. A family disintegrated because you played around with a married woman. Isn't that inconsistent with your support of family charities?"

His eyes darkened and she realized how angry he was. "While linking my scandal to a kids' camp that relies on public goodwill is consistent with *your* support of family charities."

Kate gave up any pretense of dancing. "How like a man to evade responsibility by shifting the blame."

"And how like a woman to jump into a situation she doesn't understand, and start moralizing."

They stood glaring at each other, both breathing hard. Behind Jordan, a woman laughed nervously, and Kate woke to her surroundings. The couples around them were barely moving, too busy listening with unabashed interest.

Horrified, she glanced toward the bar. Peter still sat there, engrossed in conversation. "We're making a scene," she hissed.

"What?" Jordan stared at her, incredulous.

"A scene. We're making a scene." Kate indicated the surrounding couples.

He crossed his arms. "I'm not finished."

CHAPTER THREE

"LOOK," SHE SAID through gritted teeth, "I'll hear you out. But not here. I don't want Peter's boss seeing his employee's girlfriend squabbling with a client."

With a sharp glance Kate couldn't interpret, Jordan placed a hand under her elbow and steered her through an adjacent set of French doors.

The night had grown cool and the terrace was empty; white chairs tilted forward against abandoned tables. Wisps of gray cloud, backlit by the full moon, mounted forces for an early autumn storm.

For a moment they stood in silence, looking down into the garden, where the plants took on mysterious shapes in the moonlight. Warily, Kate turned to face him.

"What do you want, Jordan, an apology? A retraction? You won't get one."

"A promise. Say what you like about me… 'Tarzan in need of a haircut'…hell, I don't care. Public opinion has never concerned me. But don't make a connection with the camp again."

Kate stiffened. That sounded suspiciously like a threat. "The behavior of anyone involved in a charity must be open to public scrutiny. You must have known that when you had the affair."

He made an impatient gesture. "I didn't know I was *having* an affair. Penny told me she was separated."

"And you believed her?"

"I don't lie and I don't expect other people to." He had the ability to come across as terribly sincere. But that didn't mean it was real.

"Will she verify your story?"

"Strangely, she's reluctant to acknowledge herself as a liar as well as an adulteress," he said dryly.

Kate's tone matched his. "So there's only your word for this new twist?"

"You know why you're reacting so badly to all this, don't you?" Jordan asked conversationally. "I've disappointed you." She blinked. "You're disappointed," he continued, "because despite our skirmishes, you've always liked me. Go with that instinct."

"Actually, I've *never* liked you."

For a moment Jordan stared down at her, his expression inscrutable. "So as well as throwing down the gauntlet professionally, you're denying we have an attraction?" He reached out to cup her chin.

His eyes, as he looked into hers, held a challenge at once compelling and terrifying. Kate had thought living with her father had immunized her against the wiles of unpredictable charmers. She'd been wrong. "You should be with me," Jordan said.

She jerked away. "Let me get your seduction technique quite clear. You try and intimidate me into keeping quiet over your sordid affair with a married woman, and then you *proposition* me?"

Jordan laughed, and it was fortunate they were outside, the sound was so loud. Kate stared at him, torn between getting away from this madman and choking the life out of him.

With a last chuckle he looked at her, his eyes gleaming. "I guess you have a point. I'm normally quite good at this."

"I'll add 'Casanova' to the list—after 'intimidating thug.'"

"Let me start again," he said quietly. "I trusted a woman I shouldn't have. But it was a mistake and I'm gutted by the impact on her family, which is why I haven't compounded their misery by publicly calling their mother a liar." He took a purposeful step closer. "Anything else?"

Kate struggled to return some sanity to the conversation. "You hardly *know* me."

"Not yet," admitted Jordan. "But I want to know you. Very well."

"You want to sleep with me, you mean." The man was insufferable.

His gaze swept over her like a blue searchlight. "Hell, yes."

She blushed, despite herself. "Are you always this direct?"

"When my instincts are this strong."

"Dogs follow their instincts. Sensible people temper instinct with reason."

"Sensible people tend to focus on reasons *not* to do things, which leads to very boring lives. Do you lead a boring life, Kate?"

She slipped back into the concealing shadows. "That's beside the point. I'm not attracted to you."

"You know, I'm getting pretty sick of you denying it." He reached for her and pulled her close, and she wondered how she'd ever misread any expression of Jordan's as guileless. She dragged herself away from him, appalled at the heated charge she felt at his touch.

"Electric, isn't it?" he said. "Makes you

wonder what it would be like if we did this." Strong arms closed around her, and his mouth took hers in a scorching kiss. Kate's heart pounded until she was deaf to everything but its frantic beat. She opened her mouth to him, unable to resist.

Other senses kicked in. The smell of him, healthy male mixed with citrus. The feel of him, hard muscle beneath his silk shirt, his long hair touching her bare shoulders.

And, dear heaven, the taste of him, and the way he moved his mouth against hers. She had never felt lust like this. It was wonderful.

It was horrible.

Kate wrenched away and, breathless, stumbled to the stone balustrade for support. Other sounds reasserted themselves—the bass beat of the music, the distant clink of glasses and chatter of conversation.

How could she have so forgotten herself here? Anyone could have seen them. Peter included.

She spun around and glared at Jordan.

That she should be reduced to acting like some cheap slut in public, and by such a man…!

In the moonlight, his white shirt glimmered as she watched him struggle to bring his breathing under control. Kate couldn't read his expression.

"Come home with me."

She steeled herself against the husky invitation. "This is yet another attempt to stop me from writing about the camp, isn't it?"

It was the wrong thing to say. He stiffened and moved back into the light, where she could see him clearly. "You're right," he said coolly, "we do need to get to know each other better first. I could threaten your boyfriend's job, I could scare you with lawyers, I could pull Triton's advertising from the paper if you connect me with the camp again…. Yes, I've thought of—"

"You can't intimidate me." She turned to go, determined not to let him see how badly he'd unsettled her.

"But I'm not going to do any of that,

Kate, because I believe in your integrity, and I know when you've calmed down you'll give me the benefit of the doubt."

She slammed the glass door behind her and walked to the bar on shaky legs. Peter dropped an arm lightly around her waist and kept talking to his boss, Brian, about rewriting software to take into account changes in taxation law. When Jordan came inside, Kate moved closer to Peter, anchoring herself to his solid familiarity.

Across the room, Jordan smiled.

"Are you okay?"

Kate loosened her grip on Peter's arm and nodded, watching Jordan leave. With a sigh, she turned to her boyfriend. "I'm a little tired." And she was. Suddenly exhausted.

He massaged her neck, knowing exactly where the sore spot was. "I should take my girl home," he said to Brian, and his habitual devotion nearly made Kate weep.

"When are you two setting a date?"

Brian had been asking the same question for three years, about as long as Peter had.

"No time like the present," Kate heard herself say.

Peter stared at her. "Are you serious?"

She took a deep breath. "Yes. Let's get married and live happily ever after."

Delighted, he leaned forward and kissed her, then pulled back in surprise at her passionate response. "Whoa there, Brian's got a pacemaker."

"Never mind that," said his boss, "let's get the champagne in."

Kate buried her face in Peter's shoulder and closed her eyes. The kiss had been nice, familiar and comforting.

She was safe.

"DIDN'T YOU SAY you'd dealt with this, Jord?" Luke strode into Jordan's kitchen and threw the newspaper on the table. One look at his weary partner and Jordan headed to the fridge, handed Luke a medicinal beer, then gestured to a stool at the island counter.

"Sit down. You look beat." He went back to turning steaks in the marinade. "How's life in Beacon Bay?"

"Insular." Luke drained half the can before he spoke again. "I'm still getting a hard time from the council, and we can't find enough tradesmen, so I've been helping out at the building site."

He held out his hands, blistered and callused. Jordan cast them a cursory glance, more intent on scrutinizing his friend's face. The terrible bleakness that had marked it since his divorce had disappeared.

Satisfied, he reached for his own beer. "You're a goddamn wimp, Carter."

"As opposed to having a future in shampoo commercials?" Luke gestured to the newspaper. "No direct references to Camp Chance, but Ms. Brogan's second character assassination—hilarious though it is—still doesn't reflect well on a trustee of a kids' camp. And we need credibility with the locals—" Luke stopped abruptly. "What *is* that bloody noise…a cat?"

"Yet another reason why Christian and Kez should have made *me* godfather of that baby and not you. At least I recognize the species."

"They wanted a role model for their daughter, not a partner in crime," retorted Luke. He crossed to the ranch slider and opened it. The two men winced as the thin howl gathered volume.

"Kezia's out buying colic powder," Jordan explained.

The crying grew louder as Christian came into sight, dark hair disheveled, blue eyes desperate. Tiny feet sticking out from the pink bundle against his shoulder pummeled his ribs.

"I've run out of options."

"Give her to me." Awkwardly, Luke took the baby and started jiggling her, using muscles that had once powered him to swimming glory. The baby's cries petered out to surprised hiccups. Luke grinned at Jordan. "Who's the perfect godfather now? Huh? Huh?"

Hiding a smirk, Jordan gathered lettuce, cucumber and tomatoes and started making a salad.

Christian raked a hand through his tousled hair, making it worse, and retrieved his soda, sitting neglected on the bench. "Okay, where were we? Oh yeah, working out what to do about Kate Brogan."

Jordan picked up his beer, took a reflective sip. He still couldn't believe how badly he'd mishandled the situation, but Kate's 'I don't fancy you' bullshit had provoked him to prove otherwise. "The fiery, feisty, infuriating and fabulous Kate Brogan."

Christian choked on his soda. "Don't tell me you've got the hots for the enemy?"

Picking up a knife, Jordan quartered a tomato with deft strokes. "Don't panic, she thinks I'm an immoral, arrogant, lunatic."

"Two out of three ain't bad." Luke stopped jiggling the hiccuping baby. "I assume your arrogance stopped you from clarifying the third?"

"Actually, I tried, but her disapproval

extends beyond Penny to my lifestyle."
Jordan savored another sip of beer. "Still,
I've never liked the pursuit to be too easy."

"You and your bloody challenges,"
complained Luke. "The camp's too important to…oh, crap!" Little Maddie had
puked on her godfather's black T-shirt.

"Actually, that's the other end," Jordan
said helpfully, but Luke didn't hear
because Maddie had started to wail again.
For a minute or two there was chaos while
he and Christian attempted to mop up.

Slicing through the cucumber, Jordan
started humming.

Sheepishly, Luke gave the disgruntled
baby back to Christian, who returned to
pacing. "Yeah, darling," he crooned, "tell
Daddy all about how stupid Uncle Jordan
thinks with his—"

"I'm back." Kezia dropped the
shopping bags. "Oh honey, you have
worked yourself up, haven't you?"

"Yeah, I have," said Christian. He
kissed his wife, relinquished the howling

baby and turned back to Jordan. "Listen, muttonhead, this project is too important to jeopardize on the first woman who doesn't find you irresistible."

Patting the whimpering infant's back, Kezia turned toward them, her expressive brown eyes wide. "This sounds serious."

Ignoring the snorts from his two friends, Jordan saluted her. "At last, someone who gets it."

"The day you settle down is the day I'm your chief bridesmaid," Christian said.

Jordan frowned. "Not *that* serious."

Kezia went into the kitchen and, with easy familiarity, found a teaspoon and gave Maddie her medicine. Only half joking, she asked, "Could she be 'the one,' Jord?"

Only half serious, he answered, "That depends—"

"On whether she puts out," Luke murmured, and he and Christian laughed.

Jordan turned his back on them and spoke to Kezia. "We have a couple of…*issues,* I think you women call it, to work through."

"She hates him," Christian explained.

"She thinks he makes a habit of seducing married women," Luke added.

Trying not to laugh, Kezia handed Maddie back to her father. "Stop exaggerating."

Jordan crumbled some feta into the salad. "And then there's the boyfriend."

"Oh," said Kezia faintly.

"So, yes," he admitted expansively, picking up the knife and a bunch of basil, "a few issues."

"Here's another one." Luke grabbed the discarded newspaper and thumbed to the classifieds. He shoved the engagement section under Jordan's nose. *Peter Walker and Kate Brogan are delighted to announce...*

"Son of a bitch." Jordan dropped the knife in the sink and stuck his finger under the running water, watching his blood swirl down the plug hole.

"This *is* serious, isn't it?" Luke asked in awe.

"Nothing a plaster won't fix." Grabbing a paper towel, Jordan wrapped his finger, then turned to see Christian standing next to an old-fashioned pistol wall mounted behind glass. His friend reached for the little steel hammer beneath the inscription, *In case of emergency, break glass.* "Don't even think about it," Jordan growled.

"'If a woman ever reduces me to your state, shoot me,'" Christian quoted. Jordan had said that a year earlier, when Christian had been in emotional meltdown over Kezia. He and Luke still argued over which of them got to pull the trigger when the time came.

"I'll never be as pathetic as you were." Jordan looped his arm around Kezia. "Have I told you how pathetic he was?"

"Many times." She smiled across the room at her husband. "But I never get tired of hearing it."

"You'll keep, wife." Christian's gaze was full of lazy promise. Maddie started to cry again.

While her parents attended to her, Luke turned to Jordan. "So back to this column… What now, hotshot?"

"Did she mention the camp? No." Jordan tossed the offending newspaper in the trash. "Problem solved." His mind was still on the engagement. He should have told Kate about how Peter had spoken about her writing; she would never have tied herself to such a loser. "For Pete's sake, give me that baby."

He took Maddie and turned her so that her little belly pressed against his palm. With the other hand, he rhythmically patted her back as he started a circuit around the dining room table. He was the oldest of a large family, and two of his sisters had kids. But babies were his favorite.

Gently, he kissed Maddie's flushed cheek. "Luke, go grill the steaks on the barbecue. Christian, make the dressing for the salad. Kez, pour yourself a glass of wine and put your feet up."

Recognizing an expert, Maddie stopped

crying and, with a tremulous sigh, closed her eyes. Jordan swung around the curve of the table and started back. All three adults were staring at him.

"Amateurs," he confided to Maddie.

CHAPTER FOUR

"I WANT YOU TO APOLOGIZE to Jordan King."

Looking at Peter's set face across the café's Formica table, Kate's heart sank. Although she'd known Peter would be unhappy when he read her second Jordan King column.

She pushed away her croissant and gave him an abridged version of the skirmish at the party, leaving out the kiss. "I can't let him think he's intimidated me. Surely you can see that?"

"What I *see* is a woman whose ego is threatening my career." Peter ran a hand through his hair, unwittingly teasing it into spikes. Everything about him bristled with disapproval.

"How can you suggest I write that

column for personal glory? It allows me to make a positive contribution to society."

"By attacking the man whose money will pay for our wedding and our house? It took me two years to win Triton over. I won't give that up for anything…or anyone."

Kate tried to get her bearings. "Please be on my side, Peter."

"Of course I'm on your side—" he took her hand and she sagged with relief "—when you behave sensibly. Obviously, you can't admit your mistake in print, but you can apologize in person."

Kate withdrew her hand. "Does my integrity mean nothing to you?"

"Does my job mean nothing to *you?* You know the only reason Brian's considering letting me buy into his company is because I secured the Triton deal." Her upset must have shown on her face, because he softened his tone. "What's going on, Kate? You used to be able to compromise."

She wanted to tell him everything, but

then her fiancé would confront Jordan and that would definitely jeopardize his contract. "I'm still the same person, Pete," she said, but the words rang hollow.

"I need more coffee." A few feet away, he hesitated, before adding, "Make the right choice, Kate. Please."

Life turned on a phrase sometimes, she thought numbly, watching him line up at the counter.

Logic, common sense, even their history reassured her that marrying Peter was the right thing to do. But…

But.

Was it fair to get engaged when her emotions were in such turmoil? These days she felt unsettled and…sullied. Even her decision to conceal the full story was tainted by the awareness that, if she told her fiancé everything, she'd have to confess she'd kissed Jordan back. That she'd felt far more for Jordan than she ever had with Peter.

Kate realized she was tearing her

uneaten croissant to shreds, and covered the mess with a napkin.

She crusaded for accountability, yet she'd been shirking it in her personal life. *That* was why she felt dirty. Because of that kiss alone, she had no right to propose to Peter, or to be using him as a safety net. The knowledge had hit her within an hour of their engagement, but she'd gone through the motions of accepting congratulations, putting the notice in the paper, choosing the ring. Pretending nothing had changed.

She held out her hand, watched the diamond on her finger sparkle. *Make the right choice, Kate, please.*

There is no choice.

Swallowing hard, Kate slipped the ring off her cold finger and laid it on his place mat. She wanted to run, but sat tight. Peter came back and handed over her cup. Then he saw the ring, and the coffee spilled into the saucer. "Okay, now this is a complete overreaction—"

"I'm sorry," she said in a rush, "this is all my fault. I'm not ready for a commitment."

He sat down hard in his chair. "But you proposed to me."

Kate tried again. "I know, and I don't want to lose you. But I…I need more time."

Peter stared at her. "We've been dating for years."

"It's not a breakup, Pete," she said desperately. "It's only a…a postponement of an engagement." Oh God, she was making a complete and miserable mess of this. "Let's just go back to the way things were."

"But we've told everyone—family, friends, colleagues, clients." His bewilderment gave way to anger. "There's even been a notice in the bloody national paper."

Kate swallowed. "We'll still be dating."

"Which makes it appear even weirder that you're breaking off the engagement."

"If it helps," she said miserably. "I'll tell everyone I'm the bad guy."

"So I get the pity vote. Oh, this just gets better and better."

Not knowing what else to say, Kate bowed her head.

For long minutes there was only the sound of Peter drumming his fingers on the table. "Okay," he said at last, "here's what we're going to do."

She looked up hopefully.

"We're going to stay engaged for another month, until my shareholding in Brian's company is confirmed. That also removes the farcical aspect of this whole thing." He shoved the ring across the table. "At the end of the month, we're going to announce an amicable parting of the ways. But right here, right now, let's you and I get something straight. We're finished."

"Don't," she said. "We can get through this."

"I've given you so much," he said, "so much, Kate. I stuck with you through your dad's disgraces, through coming second to your bloody siblings, through the rise of your career—and, incidentally, your ego— even through your attacking my best client. Now you want to publicly humiliate me."

It wasn't true. The giving hadn't been one-sided. Kate thought of the interminable work functions she'd attended; the deals Peter had made as a result of her growing reputation; the huge efforts she'd made with his dysfunctional family. She wanted to protest, but then she thought of her response to Jordan's kiss and said nothing. Numbly, she picked up the ring and put it back on her finger. He was right; it was over. She'd do what she could to mitigate his embarrassment.

Peter stood up. "For the next month, we'll be too busy working to see each other…maybe the breakup can be attributed to that. I'll think about it and let you know." He threw a bill on the table and picked up his coat.

"Don't let us end like this, Peter. Please." They'd known each other for twelve years, been each other's safe haven.

Without a moment's hesitation, he left.

Kate was in the car park when the shaking started. She fumbled to unlock her car door, scrambled in and gripped the steering wheel to steady herself, but she couldn't stop the tears streaming down her cheeks. Everyone she cared about was leaving her.

She dug into her handbag for tissues and dried her eyes, then flipped down the visor and checked her face in the tiny mirror. For once she wished she carried more makeup. No Use Crying Over Spilt Milk had been her mother's motto. Mop Up as Best You Can and Get On With It.

On her way to work Kate stopped at a gas station and used their restroom to splash cold water over her eyes. She'd give anything to go home right now, but she wouldn't shirk her responsibilities, unless she was really sick.

Sick at heart didn't cut it.

THE BOYS WERE NOT AMUSED.

Jordan saw that at a glance when he

returned from lunch with Meg, to find his two partners waiting for him at reception, their expressions grim.

"You're in trouble," murmured his secretary.

"You tackle the one on the left, I'll take the one on the right," he suggested, and startled his fifty-five-year-old assistant into an ill-advised laugh.

The faces of his two friends darkened. "For God's sake, Meg, don't encourage him," snapped Christian.

If Christian couldn't see a funny side, then something was seriously wrong. Jordan glanced at Luke's clenched jaw, and without another word, beckoned them toward the boardroom.

Christian barely waited until the door was shut. "I had a call from social services. All this negative publicity around your, quote, 'home-wrecking affair' unquote, is giving them second thoughts about the camp."

Jordan frowned. "Did you explain the situation?"

"Yeah, and they don't care. What they want is damage control—and fast."

Shit. "But she only wrote one column… one making the link. The second was tongue-in-cheek."

"Social services don't have a sense of humor. All they see is that an influential columnist from a reputable paper doesn't like you."

"If you recall, we did try and tell you that," said Luke grimly. "You're also front page news in Beacon Bay." He thrust out a faxed copy, and Jordan read the headline with a sinking heart: Camp Trustee's Ethics Called into Question. Luke started pacing the boardroom. "And you know some locals already oppose having so-called delinquents staying nearby."

Jordan's hesitation lasted a split second. "Then I'll resign as trustee," he said, giving no hint of what the offer cost him. He turned and poured a coffee.

"We thought of that," Christian admitted from behind him. "But your resignation now would be an admission of guilt, and you're not guilty."

"I can live with that," Jordan insisted.

"Besides…" Christian continued as though he hadn't spoken "…you'd still be the other trustees' business partner and friend—"

"And those links can't be severed," finished Luke.

Jordan swallowed a lump in his throat. He didn't give a damn about his reputation, but he cared about theirs. And he cared about the camp. It had begun as Luke's project; both he and Christian had survived terrible childhoods and wanted to use some of their wealth to help kids in the same predicament.

Though a passionate supporter, Jordan had always felt something of a fraud. He was the oldest of five in a close-knit family, and the only tragedy to touch his life had been his father's death when Jordan was twenty.

From birth he'd been the golden boy—

he'd even won a university scholarship before building his multimillion-dollar business. Maybe that's why he was so careless of public opinion. Now a series of stupid choices threatened not only a cause that was hugely important to his best friends, but a project that could offer hope to hundreds of needy kids.

Nothing mattered now but the fix. "Okay," he said gruffly, "here's my plan B."

CHAPTER FIVE

"YOU WANT AN INTERVIEW, I'm here to offer you one."

Kate relaxed in her chair. She'd been bracing herself for another tirade. Though she'd die before she'd let Jordan know it. He *did* scare her. But not with his outrageous demands.

No, what frightened her was her body's traitorous response to him. Even now, verging on loathing him after what his kiss had cost her, she'd found her pulse quickening when he'd sauntered uninvited into her office.

"The office for bad jokes is down the hall," she muttered, too bruised and battered to be clever right now. Then she saw his expression and her eyes widened.

"You're serious." Every journalist in the country wanted to talk to this man. "What are you up to?"

Jordan raised his hands, palms up. "There's no pleasing you, is there?" He pulled up a chair and sat down. "I also wanted to apologize for the other night." He smiled so beautifully that he only needed little angels playing harps around his head to make him appear more saintly. The smell of rat got stronger. "I'm taking a couple of kids canoeing on the Whanganui River to test it as a possible activity for the camp. Come with us."

Kate gave him her best basilisk stare; his expression remained guileless. Maybe she was being paranoid. "Well, I guess I could spare a half day," she said cautiously. Opening her desk drawer, she grabbed her diary.

"Actually, it's five days," he replied firmly.

Kate's professional interest wavered under a stronger instinct for self-preservation. But she didn't want to lose the interview altogether. "My schedule doesn't allow for trips…but I can find time for a long lunch."

"Don't worry, I've already cleared it with your editor."

The penny finally dropped. Kate picked up her pen and started playing with it. She didn't want to believe she'd been sold down the river. "And if I conclude you're still a moral vacuum?"

"You won't," Jordan replied confidently. "Besides, strictly speaking, you're not writing about me. You're writing about the work I'm doing with Camp Chance."

"Am I," she said in a dangerous voice.

"And your publisher thinks it's a great idea."

"Does she?" Kate leaned forward. "Tell me, Jordan," she said softly, "how it is that last week you told me all the strings you could pull, but wouldn't, and now, a week later, you're pulling them? How is it—" she pinned him with her gaze "—that last week you believed in my integrity, which, incidentally, did allow me to give you the benefit of the doubt when I calmed down, and now you're trying to compromise the very integrity you so admire?"

He didn't look away. "I haven't pulled any strings other than informing your editor and your publisher that I'm available."

"You know—" Kate sat back in her chair "—you can remove every doubt I have about *your* integrity by getting up right now and leaving my office."

He did stand up, but only to walk to the window. With his back to her, he said brusquely, "I'm afraid this has gone past what you and I want."

"Fine. If you won't go, I will." Getting up, she walked out of the room.

"Kate, let me explain," Jordan called after her.

Her father used to say that. Kate kept on walking.

In the staff room, she jerked her head toward a table of colleagues by way of greeting, then got her mug from the pantry. She was so angry, her hand trembled over the selection of tea bags. Kate opted for calming chamomile, jammed one into the mug and filled it with boiling water.

"We haven't finished," Jordan said from behind her, and she jumped.

Kate stabbed at the tea bag with a spoon until it sank, then turned around and said loudly, "It seems to me you have a problem with the big *N-O,* Mr. King. I'm the only woman who hasn't been suckered in by the phony charm, and you can't stand it." As she'd intended, there was a stir of sideways glances. Now he'd back off.

"Then why did you kiss me last week?" he challenged.

Kate led the way back to her office and slammed the door behind him. "Get out of my life."

"Point of order, before you get all pious about my integrity, lady. After what happened between us, getting engaged to Peter wasn't only dishonest, it was dishonorable."

She clenched her fists. "The only dishonorable thing I've ever done was let you kiss me that night…another corruption coup for Jordan bloody King."

"I'm not here to *fight* with you!" Jordan realized he was shouting, and struggled to regain control. He hadn't intended to bring up the engagement, because he knew she'd get defensive. But the way she kept looking at him, as though he was something she'd stood in, infuriated him.

"The camp's at a critical stage of the approval process, and your column made social services jumpy. A positive follow-up would make a huge—"

"So finding yourself without a reputation, you want to bum a ride on mine. Well, it's not for sale. You slept with a married woman. You kissed me knowing I had a boyfriend."

"And you kissed me back," he reminded her, holding in his temper. "Which just goes to show that people sometimes do things they regret. You know I didn't think she was married, and as for our kiss, I wouldn't have given in to temptation if your boyfriend hadn't already proved himself an asshole by…" He stopped himself just in time. In her mood, she'd kill the messenger.

Her expression grew intent. "By…?"

"Nothing." Jordan turned away.

"Well, I hate to tell you this, but schmoozing with my editor and publisher won't get you anywhere. My contract gives me power of veto."

His frustration got the better of him again. "Even if I was morally bankrupt, who suffers if social services pulls the plug? Me? No. The kids."

She hadn't expected it to go that far; he could tell by the dismay on her face. "Is that really what they're threatening?"

"Yes."

Kate folded her arms. "Then the solution's obvious. Resign as trustee."

"My ties to the camp are too complicated for that."

"Damn it," she cried, "this is emotional
blackmail." Kate turned her back on him
and stared out the window. Jordan held his
breath and waited.

"Okay," she said at last, through gritted
teeth. "I'll come."

Thank you, God.

She turned around, stabbed him in the
chest with her finger. "But if at the end
of five days I still think you're a lousy
person to be involved in a kids' camp,
I'll write that."

Jordan nodded. *No arguments now, you
sweet, sweet woman, and none for five days.*

"Deal?"

He took a deep breath. How hard could
it be to get this woman to like him?

"Deal," he said.

When he'd left, Kate turned back to the
window. Outside, a brisk wind rustled the
leaves of the maple, stark and solitary on
the inner-city street. She pressed her

hands across the cold pane, then rested her head against the cool glass.

Her life had been so orderly just ten days ago. Scrupulously tidy, with the past diligently polished to a reflective shine, showing her only what she wanted to see. One lousy newspaper column and a kiss… and now she was committed to a river trip with a man she wished to God she'd never set eyes on.

"Are you okay?"

Hearing the concern in Lucy's voice, Kate pushed back from the window. "Hey, you. Yep, absolutely fine." Avoiding meeting her best friend's eyes, she went back to her desk and picked up her handbag. "Let's go," she said brightly. If she'd remembered they were going for a drink after work she would have canceled.

Lucy put an arm around her shoulders. "What's the matter, hon?"

Kate's throat tightened. On the other hand, she really needed a friend right now.

THE CLOCK IN THE BAR chimed eight and, as if on cue, Lucy leaned across the table. One elbow missed the tabletop and they both laughed. Kate realized her friend was tipsy and, looking at her own empty glass—their third round—she decided she must be, too.

Confiding to Lucy that she'd kissed Jordan back had been a mistake. Her best friend had never liked Peter, and while she was full of sympathy for Kate's heartbreak, she saw no reason why Jordan—now that the moral issue had been cleared up to Lucy's satisfaction—couldn't help her get over him.

"Obviously, Jordan King's not husband material," she repeated. "But as I've said before, you need fun in your life."

"Who does he remind you of?" Kate said abruptly.

Lucy looked blank.

"Let me paint you a picture. Someone handsome and charismatic, popular with the ladies—too popular. Unreliable, self-

indulgent, careless of people he loves…
his kids, his wife." She watched comprehension dawn on her friend's face.

"Jordan King reminds you of your
father?"

"Reminds me?" With a bitter laugh,
Kate picked up her glass. "Haunts me,
more like. A playboy holds no appeal for
me, Luce. I grew up around a dynamic,
exciting man, and charm wears thin when
there are bills to pay. When a man cares
more about satisfying his appetites than he
does about the well-being of people he
supposedly loves."

Her voice hardened. "I've done that to
death, and there's no way I'll *ever* do it
again. Give me a man who works hard, is
faithful, pays his bills and has no imagination for sin." She swirled the red wine
in her glass. Feeling a surge of grief, she
put it down. *Oh, Pete.*

Lucy reached over and squeezed her
hand, and Kate noticed her friend's eyes
were moist. She forced a smile and sat

back, signalling the waiter for coffee. "I'll get over it," she said. "I will." If she said it enough times… Kate sighed. "Given everything, the big question is can I keep an open mind about Jordan King?"

She lifted her eyes to Lucy's. "I'd like to think I'm still big enough to do that, but…"

The waiter delivered their coffee, and Kate paused until he left. "I haven't liked what I've learned about myself over the past week, and I don't know anymore, Luce. I just don't know."

DARLING GIRL.

Cliff sat on the front step of his bungalow with a South Sea mistral leathering his already weather-beaten face and chewed his pen. Now what? The surf breaking on the coral reef beyond the lagoon caught his eye, and he wrote, *The wind direction could be good for fishing later.*

Fay came out onto the deck, wrapped in one of her hand-painted pareus, and he allowed himself to be distracted by its vibrant crimson and azure.

Most Europeans wore pareus with a tourist's self-consciousness, but Fay moved with the graceful assurance of a local. Her hair—bleached by sun and peroxide—was still damp from her recent shower.

She picked a golden-hearted frangipani from the tree beside the deck. Then teased him by tucking it behind her left ear, signaling her availability, though she'd lived as his wife for close to four years.

Cliff regularly asked her to marry him, but she always refused. "With your track record? You've got to be kidding." She would never be a woman he could take for granted; it was one of the things he loved about her.

She gave him a coquettish look that sat surprisingly well on a woman past sixty. "Write your letter."

Obediently, he looked down. *My darling girl...*

By Cliff's count, he'd written some

eighty letters over the past seven years. And though they returned like homing pigeons, he liked to write each one as though a dialogue had continued unbroken over the years of estrangement.

Since I last wrote, Fay and I have moved. We're now renting a bungalow on Muri Beach, only twenty steps from the water.

Cliff paused to look at the lagoon, crystal clear at the shoreline, fading into sky-blue as it deepened. *You kids would love it here,* he wrote, because he was an optimist.

He picked up his pineapple juice, savored its icy sweetness before swallowing.

Given the magnitude of his task, he had to be.

CHAPTER SIX

CHAPTER SIX

STANDING BY HER CAR, jarred and dusty from driving on dirt roads, Kate took one look at Jordan's formidable back and her heart sank.

In the late morning sun, his hair shone like gold as it streamed over the collar of his Swanndri bush jacket. The set of those broad shoulders was too confident, and his deft hands securing a load in one of two canoes—bright red and already half-full of waterproof storage barrels—were brown and callused. He looked horribly, seriously virile—and that was just his back.

What the hell do you think you're doing? You hate nature in the raw, your rowing skills are nonexistent and you're scared of animals. Jordan turned and grinned. *Especially wild ones.*

The small rise on which Kate stood fell rapidly to the rough clay clearing on the steep, forested banks of the Whanganui River. Wide, black and swift, the river cut through the dense green like a superhighway, its color softening to rust-brown as it eddied into the shallows where the canoes were beached.

Camping gear lay on the grassy bank, waiting to be stowed. *I'm next,* she thought, and all the queasiness of the long drive returned.

Jordan's grin broadened. His gaze moved casually down her body, taking stock of her attire, then he started to chuckle.

It was an easy sound to listen to, lighthearted, and Kate's lips twitched involuntarily before she clamped them shut. She was already self-conscious about her clothes. The outdoor adventure specialist had assured her the lightweight pants and multipocketed blue parka were essential for such a trip, and she'd spent a fortune on polypropylene this and thermal that.

In contrast, Jordan wore old jeans softened and faded with wear, and sturdy black hiking boots. Hanging out of the pocket of the blue-and-black-checked Swanndri was a black beanie.

With a sinking feeling, Kate realized her getup only trumpeted her inexperience. The new clothes rustled as she picked her way over the loose stones. "I see I should have bought a coonskin cap."

"No need to apologize." If eyes could dance, Jordan's could've led the Bolshoi Ballet. "We'll skin a possum en route."

She bit her lip. "And cook up the rest for supper, I suppose?"

Jordan considered. "Only if it's your birthday."

Damn, she hadn't meant to smile. Reluctantly, she held out her hand, lost it in his powerful grip before pulling free. "I won't be bossed, so if you think you can strut around like Tarzan of the Jungle—"

"I have no illusions, Red, believe me."

"Brown," she corrected automatically. "My hair is brown."

He started to disagree and stopped. "You're trying to provoke me into an argument. Well, it's not going to work. The color of your hair is brown, pink or purple…whatever you like. We're here to be friends, remember?"

"You might be. I'm here to assess your true character. And right now the only thing I know for sure about you is that you're unscrupulous when you want something." *Or don't want something.* Kate looked around at the bush, which was cool, dark and deep, and shivered. "Where are the others?"

He could say she drowned, then bury her anywhere. She'd never be found.

Jordan sighed. "You keep attributing all these devious motives to me, when any of my friends could tell you subtlety and I are not acquainted. My nephew, Andrew, has taken the four-wheel drive to pick up some last-minute supplies. The other kids are due any minute." He reached out and uncrossed her tightly folded arms. "Relax, Kate, my only agenda is to charm the pants off you."

It was the worse thing he could have said. She stiffened.

"Okay, let's get one thing straight," said Jordan. "While I don't regret that kiss, I have no intention of laying a hand on you without an invitation—and even that has to be *explicit.*"

"I'm engaged now," Kate reminded him. She never had been a good liar, though, and his gaze immediately dropped to her ring finger. Empty. "I didn't want to damage it, so I left it at home." For the sake of Peter's pride, she'd maintain the charade, but Kate hated wearing the ring.

Jordan's eyes returned to hers with an indefinable expression. "Well, then, I guess you're perfectly safe, aren't you?"

To her relief, a black four-wheel drive pulled up and a kid of about seventeen climbed out. Blond-haired and blue-eyed, with the greyhound build of a teenager, he was plainly Jordan's nephew. Andrew smiled, but he ducked his head and blushed when Kate smiled back, and she realized he was shy. *Not so very much like his uncle, then.*

She wanted to be useful, but it soon became apparent that the men could load faster without her help. This pervasive sense of vulnerability so early was unnerving, she decided, shivering in the river-damp air. Her mobile phone rang and she answered it with relief. "Hello?"

"Katie, it's me."

"Danny! Is everything okay?"

He laughed and Kate laughed with him. Growing up, he'd been such a ratbag, she still reacted to an unexpected phone call as if it was an SOS.

"I've got a wife to keep me out of trouble now, remember?"

"You mean she's still there?" Danny and Roz were in the second week of their honeymoon. "What part of the high seas are you calling from?"

"The cruise ship's docked in Rarotonga. We're here for a couple of days."

There was a sheepish note in his voice she recognized. "You *are* in trouble, aren't you?"

"No, we're having a great time, only…"

"Only?"

"We ran into Dad."

Kate stared blankly at the dark, fast-moving water.

"Katie, you still there?"

"I'm here."

"He was in the bar we went to." *No kidding.* "He's settled in Rarotonga with this really nice woman—" *never short of a female* "—and they've invited us to dinner tonight."

She tried to sound neutral as she asked, "Are you going?"

He sighed. "I knew you'd be pissed. That's why I'm calling. I didn't want you thinking I'd gone behind your back."

Kate wanted to be adult about this, she really did. "You're a grown-up, Danny. You don't need my approval."

"Dad said he's been writing for years." There was a hint of accusation in his tone now. "But you've been sending back the letters unopened."

"I don't want that man in my life."

"That's fine, Katie," he said carefully, "but you don't have the right to keep him out of ours."

It took Kate a few seconds to find her voice. "But you and Courtney don't care," she insisted. "C'mon, Danny, you *never* talked about him."

"Not to you, because you always got so uptight…but between ourselves? Often."

She could find nothing to say.

"Look, none of us is perfect," he said gently. "Dad made mistakes—a lot of them—but he's still our father."

Kate resisted the urge to laugh. As the eldest, she'd protected her siblings from their father's worst excesses. Now their ignorance was enabling Danny to treat the man kindly.

"Why don't you—"

"No!" In the distance she saw Jordan glance over, and she walked farther along the riverbank. "If you want to see him…go ahead, but don't ask me to do the same." She knew she sounded judgmental, unnecessarily harsh. But if she told him why, Danny would hate their father as much as she did, and she wouldn't wish that on her worst enemy.

Kate spent the next few minutes convincing Danny she didn't consider his meeting their father a desertion. But she hung up feeling exactly that.

"PASS THE BUNJEE CORDS, will you, Andy?" Jordan had to ask twice before his nephew heard him and complied. As he used them to secure the storage barrels in the canoe, it occurred to Jordan that Andrew had been very quiet on the five-hour trip from Auckland.

Since they'd left at 5:30 a.m., he hadn't thought much about it. Now he glanced over. Yep, there was a hangdog expression on the kid's normally sunny face. An expression Jordan had seen in the mirror all week. "Woman trouble?"

"No." Then Andy blushed, confirming it. *Oh great.*

"No teen angst, mate, not this week," Jordan reminded him. "Remember, we have to make a good impression on Kate."

"Yeah, yeah, I got it."

Jordan told himself to relax. A lot depended on this trip, but he was taking two great kids in Andrew and his ex-girl-friend's son, Dillon. Okay, Dillon's friend was an unknown quantity, but Jordan was confident he could manage one brat if necessary.

He'd team the novices—Kate and Dillon's mate—with himself and Andrew in the two canoes. Dillon would paddle the kayak Jordan had given him for his twelfth birthday, trading places if he got tired.

"Hey, we're here!" Dillon yelled excitedly. "Were you getting worried?"

Jordan turned around, a big grin on his face for his favorite kid. Dillon was hanging out of the open window of an old station wagon with a kayak tied to its roof rack. The vehicle had barely stopped before the boy jumped out.

"Man, I thought we'd never get here. First Ryan called to say he couldn't come, and that made us late, and I was scared you'd think we weren't coming and go without me—"

About to hurl himself into Jordan's open arms, he stopped, his expression conflicted. Jordan knew exactly what was going through his mind—was he too old for this now? Jordan took the decision away from him by enfolding Dillon in a bear hug that swung the delighted boy off his feet. "Don't give me that too-cool-to-hug crap," he said.

Putting him back on his feet, Jordan received a look of intense dislike from the short, bald man getting out of the driver's seat. Oh, great, Dillon's father had volunteered for the drop-off.

The guy had serious competition issues, which was ironic, considering it was Jordan who had persuaded Claire to let Mike back in their son's life a year ago. Ungrateful bastard.

Jordan had bitterly regretted it ever since he'd met him. Still, he could be polite for five minutes. He gave Mike a curt nod and received one in return.

Jordan returned his attention to Dillon, who was still laughing up at him, his brown eyes wild with exuberance. Dillon lived at the other end of the North Island, so they only saw each other every six to eight weeks. "You're growing, man," Jordan said gruffly.

Dillon stood as tall as he could. "Really, you think so?"

Because he knew it was important to him, Jordan stepped back and took another look. Dillon hated the fact that the only pants that stayed on his skinny little frame were size ten, and even then he had to keep hitching them up over the satin boxers that all the kids wore.

He compensated for the size ten pants by buying size fourteen sweatshirts, which always made him look as if he'd been cut off at the knees. Jordan hid a smile. His style at least, hadn't changed. "Definitely taller," he said emphatically.

"Yeah—" the kid's shoulders slumped "—but I'm still the shortest in my class."

Jordan tried to think of a reassuring response, but since he'd always been the tallest in his class—which had its own disadvantages—he couldn't think of a damn thing.

"It's much more important to be cute than tall. Hi, I'm Kate."

Dillon brightened. "You mean with girls, right?" She nodded. "Cool."

"This is Dillon," said Jordan, amused.

"And you've got years of growing yet," she continued. "My brother was the smallest in his class until he was fifteen, and now he's over six feet tall."

Mike sauntered over. "Don't go on about it, son, you're boring everyone. Save it for family."

Jordan reduced five minutes to three. "So, Mike," he said, "how're things?"

"In the real world?" Mike considered Jordan's wealth divorced him from the concerns of the common man, conveniently forgetting that Jordan's company supported not one family but hundreds. "Well, I'm still overworked and underpaid, but at least I'm not in the papers." He held out a hand to Kate. "This is a real pleasure, Ms. Brogan." For a few minutes they chatted about her columns, while Jordan seethed.

"Well, always great to see you, Mike," he interrupted after another minute, "but we've got a current to catch." He turned to Dillon, who was bouncing around impatiently. "Since your friend couldn't make it, Dil-boy—" he glanced toward the car

"—you know that means we won't need the kayak."

"Dad's coming instead," Dillon said casually.

"No…" Jordan started to say. Kate looked at him. "Kidding," he finished lamely. "That's great…*really* great." He pumped Mike's hand, each man's grip iron hard. "Give us a chance to know each other better…. So, you done much paddling, Mike?" *And we don't mean in the sea of self-pity.*

"No, but I'm sure I'll pick it up."

Swallowing his frustration, Jordan helped Mike lift the kayak from the roof rack. "I thought your nephew, Andrew, could use this," Mike suggested, "and Dillon and I would share one of the canoes."

It made sense. The kayak required a proficient paddler. Still, for a few seconds Jordan indulged himself by imagining the kayak rolling and trapping Mike underneath. "Good idea," he said reluctantly.

Dillon's face fell, but the kid didn't say

anything. Jordan knew he'd been looking forward to being master of his own ship. "Don't worry, mate," he said, ruffling the boy's dark hair. "There'll still be opportunities for you to have a paddle."

"And much better to have your dad along," said Kate, sounding a little wistful. "I wish *I* had a dad who dropped everything when I needed him."

She smiled at Mike, and Jordan thought, *Oh, great, just what I need. An alliance between* those *two.*

He started to feel desperate, and a glance at Andrew didn't help. His nephew sat on a rock, glumly throwing stones into the water. "Snap out of it, Andy." He turned back to see Kate unzipping one of the trillion pockets on her ridiculous parka and tucking away her mobile phone. "You won't be needing that," he said. Barring one hot spot with a repeater, they were going to be out of range for most of the trip.

She looked alarmed and her grip tightened. "But I'd planned to do some work."

"Then of course, bring it along," he said smoothly.

"But it won't—" Andrew stumbled as Jordan gave him a push toward the canoe.

"Never mind that…. Okay, everyone put on their life jackets and let's get going." Once they were in the current there would be no turning back, and most of their journey was through wilderness, inaccessible by road.

This wasn't the section of river Jordan intended using for the camp, but his top priority now was closing off Kate's potential escape routes.

He started to feel more optimistic. Whatever the others did, there was still one person's behavior he had total control over. Time to begin the charm offensive.

"Kate?" Gallantly, Jordan offered her his arm and escorted her to the canoe. "Watch your step now." Out of the corner of his eye he saw Mike's lip curl. Okay, the line between charm and smarm was a fine one. He'd work on that.

Unfortunately, Kate didn't look too impressed, either. "Just think of me as one of the guys."

Easier said than done, he thought wryly, watching that sweet ass as she clambered into the canoe. Resolutely, he shoved his attraction deeper into his subconscious. There were enough things to worry about on this trip without his libido becoming involved.

And at some stage he knew he'd have to tell Kate about Peter's behavior behind her back. He couldn't let her marry that jerk.

But—Jordan moved the canoe into deep water, climbed in skillfully and picked up his paddle—he'd do it after the trip.

When she liked him.

CHAPTER SEVEN

BROW CREASED in concentration, Kate watched her paddle slice cleanly into the river, flipping like a playful fish in the clear water. Suddenly she sensed the elusive rhythm she'd been chasing—tantalizingly close. Ignoring the bulky life jacket, she swung her shoulders in careful rotation and repeated the movement smoothly. Behind her came Jordan's voice, quietly encouraging. "You've got it."

Kate let out a triumphant whoop and the next stroke slapped and wobbled as if on jelly. She refocused and the paddle found water again.

Glancing to her left she saw that Mike, sharing the other canoe with Dillon, was having similar trouble. At least it wasn't a girl thing.

Five minutes later Jordan broke into her absorption. "You can look at the scenery, too, you know. Put up your paddle for a minute, I'll keep us on course."

Obediently, she lifted her eyes and blinked.

On either side of the canoe, forested banks rose. In some places, the bush sloped gently down to small, pebbled beaches. In others, the hills looked as though they'd been sliced in half, the massive trees above their lined, sandstone faces marching almost unbroken to the skyline.

Silver ferns sheltered under towering stands of tawa, rata, rimu and rewarewa, and even the steepest cliffs were prey to clumps of tenacious moss, sedges and ferns. Ahead, the river twisted and turned, its glassy surface reflecting its surroundings in a slow-moving kaleidoscope of browns and greens.

Andrew sculled effortlessly past in the blue kayak, oblivious to the beauty around him. Something was definitely troubling that teenager.

"Aww!" Kate gasped as icy water struck her full in the face.

Mike and Dillon shot past, green ripples arrowing in their wake.

Apprehensively, Dillon looked back at Kate. He hadn't been too sure when Mike had said, "Let's put some fun in this. Give Jordan a splash." Jord loved jokes, but somehow the way Mike had said it made it sound more like a trick. "Go on, son, do it."

It had been cool, sneaking up behind them and using his paddle like a spoon to flick water. Except just as Dillon hurled it, Mike had put on a burst of speed and the water had hit Kate instead.

Oh, boy. Dillon started to feel sick. She looked kinda mad with water dripping off her hair and making marks on her nice jacket. Then she wiped her face on her sleeve and started to laugh. "Let's get 'em!" she yelled to Jordan, and they dug their paddles into the water and started chasing them.

Dillon half giggled, half gasped. "Go, Dad." This *was* fun.

"They're catching up," his father said urgently. "Harder, son, paddle harder."

Dillon gritted his teeth and did his best, but Mike's steering was still wobbly. Out of the corner of his eye he saw the other canoe's bow nudge forward, and he started to giggle. He ducked too late, and water slapped him on the back of the head and trickled down his neck.

"Gotcha!" yelled Kate.

He dropped his paddle and twisted back to look at his dad. "That was *cool* fun."

"Yeah." His dad was staring after Jord and looking kinda upset, even though he hadn't got very wet.

"It's okay," Dillon reassured him. "No one ever beats Jord unless he lets them." He looked at the man in the fast disappearing canoe, trying to find words to describe how he felt about him. "He's the best."

Dad didn't look any happier. "We lost because we're a man and a kid against two adults, that's all."

"Well, yeah." Hadn't Dad seen that Jord was doing most of the work? Dillon picked up his paddle. He used to think it would be exciting to have his father back in his life; as he'd gotten older, he'd grown curious about him. But he was finding it a little disappointing.

Not that Mike wasn't nice or anything. He always tried to arrange something fun to do together and he had rad computer games—because that was his job, computers. Mum hadn't wanted Mike back in Dillon's life to begin with, but lately that had changed. A lot. Dillon had caught them kissing last week, though they pretended he hadn't.

If Mum wanted to remarry Dad, that was fine by Dillon. He liked Mike... except when he got sad. Dillon glanced back. He looked kinda sad now, and it made Dillon uncomfortable.

"Let's catch up to Jord." Jordan was never sad.

"ANDY!" JORDAN BELLOWED, clearly frustrated. "For the last time, stay with the group!"

Oh, great, thought Jordan. *Just bloody great.*

Andrew stopped paddling, but his scowl told everyone what he thought of the idea.

His nephew was supposed to be showing Kate how well Jordan got on with teenagers.

Being charming was going down like a lead balloon with Kate, and Mike wasn't helping by snorting after every compliment.

Isn't anyone on my side?

Dillon paddled past and gave him a big smile, and Jordan's mood lightened.

"Listen up, everyone," he called. "There's a pebble beach half a kilometer downstream. We'll call it a day there."

The two canoes drew abreast of Andy's kayak. "But it's only lunchtime," Andrew complained. "Normally, we'd paddle five or six hours before making camp."

"Yeah, mate, but we've got two novices on the trip in Mike and Kate," Jordan explained patiently. "I think three hours is enough for their first day."

"He's insulting us, Kate," Mike said jovially. "Are we going to take it?"

Kate glanced over her shoulder at Jordan. "Don't hold back on my account. I exercise regularly."

Resisting the urge to say he already knew that from admiring her hot bod, Jordan processed his response through the charm filter. "You certainly seem very fit, and I think it's wonderful that you find the time with your busy schedule." Oh God, he sounded like his mother.

Looking a little startled, Kate took another couple of strokes, her paddle cutting through the water with a flourish.

"And this is easy when you get the hang of it," she conceded.

"No, you're naturally gifted." She turned away in disgust, and Jordan didn't blame her. He was starting to hate himself.

"What a greaser," Mike hooted.

I'll kill him.

Ignoring Mike, Jordan addressed Kate's back. "You might be fit, but are you paddling fit? Andy, Dil-boy and I will be okay, but if you two want my advice—"

"We don't, do we, Kate?" Mike interrupted. "Without giving her a chance to answer, he paddled alongside. "Stop being a spoilsport, King. You don't have to be in charge *all* the time, do you?" Jordan noticed Dillon looking uncertainly between them.

"Fine," he said lightly. "You set the pace today, Mike." *And live with sore muscles tomorrow, you cocky bastard. Because I'm not fighting with you in front of Kate. Or Dillon.*

If the river conditions required it, he

wouldn't hesitate in overruling Mike. But they were on a calm stretch of water. And Jordan itched to give the man a lesson in why he should obey his expedition leader. Speaking of which…

"Andy!" he bellowed. "Stay with the *group!*"

THE CANOE ROCKED unsteadily as Kate clambered onto the long shingle bank. Ignoring Jordan's proffered arm—attached as it was to an obsequious smile—she stretched her aching arms high above her head.

"I'm fine," she said firmly, crunching over the stones on legs that had somehow forgotten how to walk. "Where are the… facilities?"

All the males grinned. "You'll find a long-drop up the path to the left," said Jordan. "Grab a stick for the cobwebs if you don't like spiders."

Kate tried to look unconcerned.

"Oh, and you'll be needing this." He

unscrewed the lid on one of the water-proof barrels and tossed her a roll of toilet paper.

"Want me to check it for you first?" Dillon offered. He was such a sweetie.

"I think I'll be okay," she said, then noticed his disappointment. "Actually, I'm only pretending to be brave. Thanks, Dillon."

Delighted, he picked up a big stick. "Follow me."

Trailing the boy up the track, stomping to warn the wild animals they were coming, Kate thought, *Who am I kidding? I am pretending*. She was so far out of her comfort zone here she would have sworn she was on another planet.

She had wanted to stop for the day much earlier—her arms ached; her legs had pins and needles—but she hadn't wanted to be the girlie-girl spoiling everyone's fun.

And she didn't want Jordan to know she had a weakness; he'd just find a way of using it to his advantage. If anything, the morning had only strengthened her dislike for him. He must have a very low opinion of her intelligence if he thought he could flatter her into thinking he was a great guy. What a...a—Kate recalled Mike's term and bit her lip—*greaser.*

Her faith in Jordan's ability to lead them safely back to civilization had also been badly shaken. He'd let Mike—a beginner—tease him into relinquishing control of the schedule. From Kate's point of view, that was a crazy thing to do. And inexplicable. It was obvious the two men were jealous of each other's relationship with Dillon.

Dillon came out of the outhouse covered in cobwebs. "All clear."

Kate gulped and took the toilet paper. "You know what?" she said. "Maybe I'll go *behind* the outhouse."

"But that's where I put all the spiders." His brown eyes were very earnest. "I got rid of 'em all, I promise. Even the weta."

Knowing the native New Zealand crawler was now outside with her, Kate hurried into the dimly lit shed. The old wooden door creaked as she closed it. "Wait for me?" she whispered through the crack.

"Sure," Dillon said.

On the way back to the river she asked him how he knew Jordan.

"He dated my mum."

"Oh." Not *another* married woman. *Now, Kate,* she warned herself, *don't jump to conclusions.* "But your dad wasn't living with you," she prompted.

"Oh, no." Dillon swung on a low tree branch. "He's only been around for a year. Jord dumped Mum way before that." He let go of the branch and landed lightly on his feet. "Only I forgot that we don't call it that anymore. Now Mum and Jord say they 'drifted apart.' I wonder what's for lunch?"

"CAN I GO EXPLORING?"

Jordan looked up from repacking the remains of lunch. He'd insisted Kate sit down and rest, and Mike had taken it as an invitation to do the same. Now he and Kate were having the bonding conversation Jordan desperately needed with her.

"Sure, Dil-boy. Take your dad with you."

"He said he's relaxing."

"Okay, take Andy."

Lying outstretched on the shingle, his eyes closed, Andrew sighed. "Do I have to?"

"Yes."

Grumbling, the teenager got to his feet. Jordan steered him out of earshot. "Okay, what's this all about?"

Andy shrugged.

"You know I haven't got time for melodrama, so either spit it out or sort it out." Jordan hadn't meant to sound so harsh, but before he could qualify his statement, his nephew's mouth tightened in a stubborn line.

He stomped away, calling for Dillon. "C'mon, brat, let's get out of here."

What little sympathy Jordan had to spare evaporated. "And don't take it out on Dillon. You know he's been dying to hang out with you."

"*Fine!*" Andy yelled. He and Dillon disappeared into the bush.

"Boy," said Mike, "King's got a way to go handling teenage boys."

Though she'd been thinking the same thing, Kate gave Mike a noncommittal shrug. Tempting though it was to bad-mouth Jordan, it didn't seem fair to dump on the guy doing all the cleaning up.

"And you were right on the button when you said King's environmental interests are probably a clever manipulation of current concerns," said Mike. He seemed to know her columns word for word. "And," he continued, "I reckon those charitable donations *are* salving a bad conscience."

Kate smiled politely and picked up her book. Certainly, after today's smarminess she'd have to agree with Mike's assessment that Jordan's charm was calculated. As for his pretty boy looks… She glanced at him surreptitiously.

No, he couldn't be accused of prettiness. Too rugged for that. He radiated raw power and good health. Looking back at her book, Kate tried to concentrate.

"'His signature long hair is ridiculously affected,'" quoted Mike. "God, I loved that line."

"Am I missing anything?" Jordan asked.

Kate blushed, hoping he didn't think she'd encouraged Mike, and even Dillon's dad looked embarrassed.

"How about I go find the boys," the man suggested. "We should get going." He disappeared into the bush, and, flustered, Kate returned to her reading.

Sitting opposite from Kate, a sun-warmed boulder at his back, Jordan took the opportunity to study her.

The sun came out from behind a cloud and struck fire into her red hair, which was tousled from the morning's rigors. She was frowning slightly under his scrutiny, and her jaw was set, but the freckles across the bridge of her straight nose softened the effect.

Add the long lashes casting shadows on her pale skin and, God help him, she was almost cute. Fortunately, her sensual mouth saved her from that fate. Idly, Jordan tried to recall the exact color of her eyes.

"It's rude to stare," she said without looking up.

"What's the book?" he asked.

Reluctantly, she showed him, glancing up in the process. Her eyes were the capricious brown of the river, flecked with green.

Jordan dropped his gaze to the cover. *Predatory Porcines—When Wild Boars Attack.*

His shout of laughter echoed across the water. "Kate, I've encountered dozens, possibly hundreds of wild pigs in the bush over the years. Every single one bolted at first sight of me."

"They *are* rated as one of the more intelligent animals." Her delivery was so straight it took Jordan a second to realize he'd been insulted. He flicked her an appreciative grin, which she ignored. But there was a half smile on her lips as she skimmed back through the pages. "And I don't think you should get complacent. In chapter six, a pig hunter said he always scoffed at attack stories. Until it happened. His rifle misfired, there was no tree handy, so he had to stand his ground and fight off a three-hundred-pound boar with his gun butt." She started reading aloud, "'If you're trapped, never turn your back and run because the animal will knock you to the ground.'"

Her eyes were very bright as she slammed the book shut. "And you're as good as *dead* if the tusks hit your vital organs."

"You're not reading this stuff because you're scared," he said delightedly, "you're reading it because you're bloodthirsty. Hell, you're all but licking your lips."

She looked horrified. "Take that back!"

"You probably have a shelf full of animal-attack books."

"Four or five doesn't rate as a collection." She started to laugh. "And it's *not* because I'm bloodthirsty. I admire fortitude in adversity."

Something Jordan suspected she'd needed in her adolescence. Over the past week, he'd done his own research. He wanted to know everything about the woman he was trying to impress.

Her mother had died of cancer when Kate was sixteen. A year later she'd left school to keep house for her father and younger siblings. By all reports, her dad was a colorful character, with an eye for the ladies and an indefatigable enthusiasm for get-rich-quick investments, which had kept the family poor.

He'd gone opal mining in Australia when Kate was twenty-one, leaving his two younger children in her care. Amazingly, he'd found an opal that revived the family's fortunes and freed Kate to pursue a career.

But he'd never returned home. His children must visit him abroad, though the private investigator Jordan had hired could find no record of it. The PI had discovered that Kate had rejected two good job offers overseas—presumably to stay with her siblings, who'd only recently flown the nest.

Coming from a close family himself, Jordan imagined she was finding the adjustment hard. *Imagined* being the key word. She hid her feelings, a concept completely foreign to him.

"There's an awful section on pig hunting," she said in disgust. "Dogs are used to track and hold the boar, then the hunter slits its throat." Her eyes held an unspoken question.

"No—" Jordan picked up the thermos beside him and poured tea into plastic cups "—I don't hunt like that."

"But you do hunt?"

"With a gun, yeah." He handed a cup to Kate, who was trying not to look disapproving. "I don't care about your religion, your politics or your criminal record," he said sternly, "but if you're a vegetarian, I'm leaving you here." He loved how she bit her lip lest she encourage him by smiling.

"I eat meat if it's organic," she conceded, "and free-range poultry."

"It's always struck me as ironic that you conscience-ridden types will only eat the happiest animals."

That won a chuckle. "I never thought of it like—" Tea splashed onto the ground as she bolted upright. "Wait a minute, did you bring a gun?"

"No, I figured the temptation to shoot me would be too much for you." When she laughed, he felt as if he'd won a gold medal at the Olympics.

"You're very pretty when you smile." *I cannot believe I said that.*

Kate's warmth vanished. "The others are coming back. Shall we go?" Standing, she walked toward the river.

It wasn't yet midafternoon, but already the forest's giant trees had caught the sun and were drawing it down behind them, their long shadows creeping across the water.

Shivering, Kate tossed the remains of her tea into the river like a protective charm. "This place is almost prehistoric."

"The forest has been legally protected for over a hundred years. It's a mile deep in some places."

"The roads must be rough."

Jordan picked up the day pack and returned Dillon's wave. Mike and Andrew ignored him. "The only access is by river. At this time of the year, we'd be lucky to see a ranger."

Kate looked across at the dense bush and frowned. "So if the boat sinks, we'd have to try to find a way out through *that?*"

"Absolutely not. We'd sit tight and wait for help." He saw her alarm. "I have an emergency transmitter. It would only take five or six hours."

"And there's my cell phone," she reminded him.

He decided to get it over with. "For the most part we'll be out of range."

"But I have work to do…calls to take…. Why was none of this in the briefing notes?"

The answer—that she wouldn't have come—was so obvious Jordan didn't reply.

"Wait a minute." Her brow furrowed. "On the map you supplied, I'm sure the river had a road running alongside it."

He bent to retie his boots. "You must have misread it."

"The heavier person sits at the back. They also steer. If you're keen to learn, I'll team you up with Dillon when there's no prospect of rapids."

"Rapids!" Kate forgot her aches and pains. "How many does this river have?"

"Over two hundred, but the water level's so high with all the rain upstream they've flattened out." Jordan sounded disappointed. Kate offered up a prayer of thanks. "But that could change at any time," he added, "and then we'd have some fun."

She decided she'd had about all the fun she could take for one day. Things kept going from bad to worse. "Okay, you win. Let's park this thing and make camp."

"You're a minute too late—look around."

The gentle gradients had become buttresses defending the land. The gorge closed in, reducing the sky to a strip of fast-fading blue. In the gathering gloom, Jordan's teeth were very white. "Beautiful, isn't it." And he wasn't joking.

By the time the three craft reached a

suitable egress point, Kate was grateful for the deep twilight hiding her exhaustion.

The canoe hit the bank with a bump, and this time her body left her no choice but to accept Jordan's help. She noticed Mike was also moving stiffly, though he made no complaint, joining the others in unloading the gear. Picking up a bundle, she stumbled up the hill in their wake.

At the top, Jordan dropped the tent he was carrying and looked about him with satisfaction. "Home, sweet home."

Appalled, Kate glanced around the small clearing, which was sparsely covered with damp, rangy grass. Beyond, a dark line of trees huddled like conspirators.

"Sit down, Kate, while we unpack." Jordan's voice sounded kind, but she was too tired to differentiate kindness from sycophancy.

"No, I'll help."

He shrugged. "Okay, you and Andrew unload. Mike, you collect wood and get a fire started. Dillon and I will pitch the tents."

"I'll pitch the tents with Dillon," Mike said.

"Fine," Jordan snapped. "I'll get the wood. Andy…"

But Andrew had already disappeared. Kate followed the teen down the hill, wondering if she should ask him what was wrong. Her attempts at conversation today had been answered in monosyllables and grunts. Still, it seemed she was the only person willing to try.

She waited until they'd brought up all the gear, then followed him back down to the boats. A cold moon had risen over the forest, making stark shapes of the trees and glistening off the black water. Andrew was sitting on a boulder, with his arms wrapped around his knees.

For a moment she hesitated. This was really his uncle's job…. Then she heard a sob and forgot everything but the need to comfort. For the sake of Andrew's pride, she made a lot of noise going down, and saw him give his face a hurried wipe.

"Oh!" Kate feigned surprise. "I thought there was more gear to bring up."

"No. We're done. You can go."

Instead she joined him on the boulder. For a few moments they looked out over the water. A fish jumped, probably an eel, and Kate shivered. "It's beautiful here," she lied.

"Umm." Andrew didn't encourage her.

"Listen, I know we're virtual strangers, but if you need someone to talk to—"

"I've got Jordan."

"Yeah, well, I couldn't help notice today that…" She trailed off. What? That he'd brushed Andrew off a couple of times? Had lost patience with his nephew? Neither seemed the right thing to say.

"I know," said Andrew, interpreting her silence, "but it's because he's under pressure. Normally he's not such a…" Now it was his turn to fade out.

"Jerk?" finished Kate. Another fish splashed, closer this time, and she pulled her feet higher up the rock. "I wouldn't know," she said. "The jerk is the only guy I've ever met."

The only new thing she'd learned about Jordan today was that he didn't fight just with her, he fought with everybody. Except Dillon, and that was only because the boy thought he could walk on water. Kate was tempted to suggest Jordan try.

"He's only a jerk around you," said Andrew, suddenly fierce. "And he's nothing like the guy you wrote about in your column. He's…well, he's my hero. It sounds lame, I know."

Not lame, thought Kate. *Tragic.*

"And if he's being a jerk," Andrew continued, "it's because he has to make you like him."

"No, he doesn't," she replied quietly, and realized with relief it was true. "All he needs to do is convince me he's fit to be involved with a kids' camp. Wait a minute, didn't I come down here to give advice to you?"

At last he smiled. "I don't know you well enough to spill my guts. Sorry."

Well, that put her in her place. Using his shoulder as a prop, Kate struggled to her feet. "Fair comment. But if you want someone to talk to…"

"Thanks, but it's guy stuff." He turned back to the river, politely dismissing her. Halfway up the hill, she looked down. The plaintive cry of a morepork owl and the vast blackness surrounding the shadowy figure only accentuated the boy's isolation.

It hurt Kate to see Andrew's loneliness, and then it made her angry.

JORDAN WATCHED DILLON and Mike putting up a tent together. Of course Mike would be doing it the hard way.

Jordan dumped the bundle of firewood he'd collected in the clearing. He had no right to feel jealous; he knew that. But that didn't stop him.

Putting the pot he was holding on the camp stove, Jordan went to build the campfire. Sure, he'd supported Dillon's passionate interest in reconnecting with his father, but he hadn't done it out of altruism. He'd done it out of guilt. If Jordan had only married his mother, Dillon wouldn't have needed to scrape the bottom of the barrel for a father.

Crouching, Jordan cleared the ground around the site he'd chosen for the fire. It had taken two years of dating Claire before he'd realized he was considering marriage not because he wanted to be her husband, but because he'd love to be Dillon's dad.

And even then he'd dragged out the relationship for another year. Why the hell weren't young men given lessons in emotional intelligence? It would save young women so much grief. He sorted the wood, looking for kindling.

When he'd met Claire, her son had been two, an exuberant bundle of mischief. The day he'd had the guts to break it off had been Dillon's first day at school, and Jordan's twenty-fifth birthday.

She'd been offered a great job as a legal

secretary in Wellington, which, of course, she was going to turn down because of him—the guy with a hundred reasons why getting married *now* wasn't a good idea.

It was that day Jordan realized he couldn't keep pretending they were going to live happily ever after. It wasn't fair to Claire, whose only fault was that she relied on him for her happiness at a time when he was already buried under other obligations.

And because Claire was so great, she'd let him stay in contact with Dillon, initially, Jordan suspected, because she'd hoped he'd change his mind about marriage; and later, because she saw how much Dillon loved him. And how much Jordan loved her son.

Jordan couldn't resist calling, "You've got a loose guy rope on the left."

Mike shot him a look. "We've got it, thanks."

Jordan went back to building the campfire. Maybe he wouldn't feel so guilty if Claire had found someone else, but she hadn't. After all these years, they were good enough friends to talk about most things, but the one issue they never discussed was whether she was still in love with him.

He struck a match, and the kindling smoldered and caught. Jordan stared at the growing flames. He'd learned his lesson. He only dated women who felt the same way about commitment. Strong women he couldn't hurt.

Kate approached from the river, a martial light in her eyes, and Jordan realized that was exactly why he was so attracted to her. She fit his criteria. The knowledge came as a relief.

"Your nephew's unhappy and he needs you to listen."

"I know that," he said, curbing his irritation. *Be nice,* Jordan told himself. "He's not ready to talk."

Kate put her hands on her hips. "I said *listen,* Jordan. Maybe if you weren't so hung up on trying to impress me, you could find time for him."

Jordan narrowed his eyes. "What's Andrew been saying?"

"That you're not a jerk."

That gave him pause. "And did you believe him?"

"What do you think?" she said scornfully.

Jordan tossed the matches aside. "That trying to get you to see past your prejudices about me is a complete waste of bloody time. I've tried to be nice...."

"By insulting my intelligence with phony compliments? Mate, if you leaked any more oil, you'd be an environmental disaster."

Over by the tent, Mike laughed. "Take Dillon and collect more firewood," Jordan said to the other man. There was no room in his tone for argument.

Mike picked up a torch and the two of them left without a word. Jordan became aware that the lid of the pot on the camp stove was banging. His temper wasn't the only thing under pressure.

"The possum's trying to escape," he commented, giving the saucepan a vigorous shake as he brought it over to Kate. She shrank back when he lifted the lid, and he realized she thought he'd been serious.

"It's popcorn," he said dryly. "Comfort food to keep us going until I make dinner."

She stared at him. "You cook?"

"Did you want to add sexism to my other failings? Sorry, I can't oblige on that one." Jordan allowed himself a little sarcasm. "How does this fit with my womanizing? It must make things messy for you."

"Not at all," she replied, taking a handful of the warm, buttery popcorn. "Nothing is more seductive than a man with domestic skills. It's a mandatory part of any modern Casanova's tool kit."

She was looking at him through her rogue-tinted spectacles again. *You're not letting her provoke you into a fight.* "I'm not a Casanova," he said patiently. "Just a guy who's not ready for marriage."

"Do you tell that to the women you date?"

"Yeah, I do. Right up front, I say I travel around a lot and I'm not looking for long-term."

"A challenge like that must make you all but irresistible."

God, she was clever. He had to admit it did. "We were talking about my nephew."

"Andrew said you're trying to impress me. Stop. If you're trying to sell the real you, then have the guts to *be* the real you."

That pissed him off. "This from the woman who takes offense every time I'm honest with her."

"That's bullshit," she snapped back.

"That's the truth." He regarded her with exasperation. "If you want me to be real, then give me a fighting chance and make this a real truce, Kate, not one you're paying lip service to."

Unable to meet his eyes, she stared across the circle of firelight into the blackness. "Okay, here's a compliment—I can't believe the transformation. This place is almost homey."

"I can make a home anywhere. It's one of my things."

Envy and loneliness suddenly tugged at her heart. After her mother's death, she'd fashioned a comfort zone for her younger siblings and convinced them that work, not women, kept their father away. But for Kate, home had died with her mother. Her dream had been to make a new one with Peter.

"Cuckoos can make a home anywhere, too. They simply steal other birds' nests."

The dregs in Jordan's mug hit the fire with a hiss as he stood up. "That was a short-lived truce."

She rubbed her forehead. "You're right… I'm sorry," she said wearily. "Let's start again. I realized when I was talking to Andrew that I don't have to like you, I just have to be fair. It came as a huge relief to me."

To her surprise, Jordan laughed. "And to me, if it means I don't have to charm you."

"No. To be honest—since we're being

honest with each other now—it turns my stomach."

"It was turning mine," he admitted. "And you're not going to change your mind the first time I say something you take offense to…because you know it's going to happen, Kate."

"I don't doubt that, but I won't change my mind."

"In that case—" Jordan gestured to the food barrel "—be a good girl and peel the spuds while I go talk to Andrew."

TIRED AS SHE WAS, Kate couldn't sleep in her tiny tent. Everything ached—her body, her brain and her heart.

She hadn't thought about her personal worries all day. But now Peter and her father jostled for room in her tired mind, along with anxiety about the work commitments she couldn't meet while she was out here without a phone.

She'd been the first to call it a night after dinner, but others had quickly followed, Mike muttering something about "bloody Jordan" fixing his tent.

The boys had finally stopped grunting and snuffling outside Kate's tent. They'd found her book on porcine attacks during dinner and had been teasing her mercilessly ever since. "Guys," Jordan had warned, but he hadn't been able to stop laughing, either. The real Jordan King was definitely back.

Now, an hour later, only Jordan still sat by the fire. Thinking what, Kate wondered. Andrew had come back with him from the river, if not cheerful then at least with a teenager's appetite, which had to be a good thing.

On their return, Jordan had answered Kate's unspoken question with the tiniest nod. At least someone's problems were being resolved.

Another twenty minutes passed while she tossed and turned, trying to find a comfortable position on the thin air bed. Through the side of her tent, she watched the fire glow, then Jordan doused it and her eyes followed the flashlight as he went to bed.

She fumbled for her own flashlight, touching it for reassurance. All that stood between her and wilderness was one thin sheet of waterproof nylon. Only two separated her from the man contributing to her insomnia.

Huddling deeper in her sleeping bag, Kate suddenly remembered her jacket still hung outside. It would be saturated with dew by morning.

Reluctantly, she got out of her bag and unzipped the tent, shivering as the damp air pierced her cotton T-shirt. She scanned for wild animals then crept out into the clearing.

Jordan and Andrew's tent glowed in the darkness. She recognized Jordan's outline as he sat against his backpack, reading.

Kate retrieved her jacket and was halfway back to her tent when she remembered that wild animals could also drop from trees. Glancing up nervously, she forgot everything.

So many stars winked and twinkled in the bright stillness of the moonlit sky.

Shrugging on her jacket, Kate stared until she couldn't bear the cold any longer. Then, strangely comforted, she crawled back into her tent.

Reaching for the zipper, she saw Jordan's silhouette as he stood up. His arms crossed to grab hold of the T-shirt, pulling it up and over his head. He paused there a second, every muscular curve of his arms and upper body thrown into sharp relief.

Kate's mouth went dry.

He tossed the shirt to one side and his hands moved to the front of his jeans. His long hair fell forward as he bent to take them off, a movement that also accentuated the flat planes of his stomach, even in shadow.

Kate held her breath as he started peeling the jeans slowly down his body. So slowly, she had time to realize what she was. A voyeur.

"Are you enjoying the show, Kate?" His murmur reminded her they were the only two awake.

Horrified, she ducked back into her tent and scrambled into her sleeping bag, pulling it over her head like a cocoon.

CHAPTER NINE

DILLON ROSE at first light, hauled on his clothes as quietly as he could, and tiptoed out of the tent he shared with his dad.

He'd rather have shared with Jordan, but he knew it would hurt Mike's feelings, so he hadn't suggested it.

Passing Kate's tent, he was tempted to do some pig snorts, but he resisted it. This time alone with Jord was too precious to share with anyone else.

Jordan was already sitting on a log, waiting, two steaming hot mugs of cocoa beside him. Sharing conspiratorial smiles, they silently left camp and headed down to the river. From one of the storage barrels Jordan extracted two telescopic fishing poles and some eel bait.

Only when they sat on boulders, lines hanging in the water, did Dillon feel the tension ease from his body. He dipped his tongue in the mug, where a marshmallow melted into the sweet chocolate, and then breathed steam into the still morning air. "Hey, I'm a dragon."

Jordan did it, too, and they forgot about fishing in the heat of competition to see who could send a steam ball the farthest. Dillon won.

"You let me," he accused, wrapping his legs tighter in the blanket. The sun hadn't climbed over the forest yet and it was cold.

"Did not."

"Did, too."

"Did not."

"Now you're being childish," Dillon said with dignity.

"Am not."

Dillon grinned. "Are, too."

They fished for a while in comfortable silence, Dillon checking the bait occasionally, like Jordan had taught him. When

Dad had first offered to take him fishing, Dillon had explained, "I can do any kind—spincast, spinning, baitcast and fly. Here's a picture of me with my first fish. I caught it with Jordan on his launch."

Except Mike had looked funny and said, "Well, I guess a simple rod and reel cast over the side of a borrowed dinghy isn't going to cut it." Dillon had assured him that any kind of fishing was fine by him, but somehow they'd ended up playing computer games all weekend instead. Dillon loved it, but Mum got grumpy when she heard about it. That reminded him…

Dillon raised the question that had been bothering him since yesterday. "You don't mind that I asked Dad to come, do you? Mum thought it would be a good idea."

Jordan shot him a surprised glance. "Did she?"

"I'd rather it was just us." It seemed important Jordan know that.

Jord patted his shoulder. "Really, it's fine."

"He can be a bit…funny sometimes, but he's okay, really. I mean, do you like him?"

Jord never lied to him, so Dillon knew it was dangerous asking, but…

"I don't know him very well yet," Jordan said carefully. He changed the subject to other things—school, sport, friends—and Dillon was happy to do it. Because he was suddenly terrified that Jordan was going to ask if Mike liked *him.*

Yesterday, Dillon had realized with a horrible creeping feeling that Dad *didn't,* and Dillon didn't know what to do about it. The tension crawled back into his slight shoulders. Then an eel jerked on the hook and he forgot about everything but reeling it in.

KATE ROLLED OVER with a groan, every muscle in her arms and shoulders screaming. Her upper body had obviously been stolen in the night, beaten to a pulp and re-attached with a rusty hinge. Even her breasts were sore. Hauling herself upright, she rubbed them tentatively.

"Want some help with that?" Jordan grinned through the clear plastic window.

She scowled. "Go away." The zipper whizzed upward and the rest of him appeared, the picture of male vitality. He waved a cup under her nose…real coffee. Kate took it, biting back a yelp as her palms contacted hot metal. Jordan turned her hand over and looked at her blisters. His smile faded. "Why didn't you tell me yesterday?"

"It's no big deal, I just need a plaster." The tent felt too small with him in it. She started crawling out of her sleeping bag. "I'll get dressed."

But he was watching her pained movements. "This is my fault. I should never have let Mike goad me."

Wow, was that actually remorse she heard? Not that Kate considered herself his charge. Still, it was time some of the torture went the other way.

She injected a feeble note in her voice. "Don't worry about it." Groaning, she struggled pathetically to her feet. "Really, I'm fine." A girl didn't go to convent school without learning how martyrdom worked.

"You need a massage."

"No!" Dropping the guilt trip, Kate gritted her teeth and forced her back to straighten. "See? I'm fine." No way was he touching her after last night's awful realization that she was still attracted to him. "Paddling will loosen me up."

"That's for me to decide." He left before she could argue.

Shit! Painfully Kate pulled on clothes, twisting into them like a demented snake, and crawled out of the tent.

Camp was a hive of activity. Mike and Andrew were dismantling the tents, Jordan crouched over the stove frying breakfast, and Dillon was buttering bread. "Hi, Kate! Wanna see what I caught?"

"Sure, buddy, in a minute, hey?" All her attention was on Jordan. "Look, I've loosened up already." She swung her arms to show him. They flopped like two strands of overcooked spaghetti. Her bare foot touched something wet and slimy; Kate looked down and leaped back with an involuntary screech. An eel lay on the grass, its dead eye staring up at her.

All the guys laughed except Dillon, who dropped his knife and hurried over. "Don't stand on breakfast."

"Well, at least there's nothing wrong with your legs," Jordan commented. He looked at Mike. "You need to see this."

Mike hobbled up and Kate realized she wasn't the only one suffering this morning. His eyes widened when Jordan showed him her palms. "I'll get the first aid kit," Mike offered.

"Next time," Jordan said, "don't argue with me."

The other man stopped in his tracks. "Are you saying this is my fault?"

"Our fault, yeah."

"Well, I won't accept it. Like you said,

you're the leader. The buck stops with you, not me."

"Dad," Dillon said, clearly scared.

"It's okay, Dil-boy," Jordan said quietly. "Mike and I just needed to get something clear. I think we've done that now, haven't we, mate?"

"Oh, yeah, you're the big—" Mike saw Dillon's face and stopped. His son was near tears. Mike thrust out a hand, and Jordan shook it. "Yeah, mate, we're sorted. Dillon, come help me fix Kate up."

The boy was desperately trying to control himself. Kate wailed as plaintively as she could, "We're not *really* having eel for breakfast, are we?"

Dillon's sob came out as a laugh. "You're such a *girl*."

"I know," she said meekly. "But I really am trying to be one of the guys."

"Breakfast will be ready in ten minutes," Jordan called after them, adding ominously, "and then we'll discuss that massage, Kate."

She didn't answer, following Mike to where his gear was stowed. He sat her on Dillon's rucksack, produced a comprehensive first aid kit and started dressing her hands with a competence she hadn't previously seen in him.

Dillon didn't hang around long. He'd hoped for blood or open wounds, he told Kate cheerfully as he left. She and Mike exchanged grins. "Great kid," she said.

"Not due to me, I'm afraid. His mother raised him."

"I'm sure he inherited something from you."

"Yeah—" Dillon's twinkle suddenly appeared in Mike's brown eyes "—his height."

It was the first time she'd seen his sense of humor. He must've noticed her surprise.

"I am a nice guy, really," he said. "Being around King always brings out the worst in me."

Kate found herself in the interesting position of being in complete sympathy with Mike, yet needing to defend Jordan for Dillon's sake. "I think…" she began vaguely, then stopped. "You need to find something in common."

"I'm a poorly paid computer technician whose most exciting hobby is gardening. He's a millionaire entrepreneur who excels at extreme sports. You find it."

There was silence for a few minutes as Kate racked her brains. Mike finished covering her blisters with a protective plaster. "I know who I'd choose if I were a twelve-year-old boy," he said.

Dillon ran over. "Breakfast is ready." He giggled. "Kate, we saved you the head."

She pressed the back of her hand against her forehead. "I think I'm going to swoon."

He hooted; Mike chuckled. They wandered back, Kate trying to appear supple and loose limbed. Mike stopped her before they got within earshot. "Hey, I'm really sorry for yesterday. I can see you're in a lot of discomfort."

"Shh," she replied. "I'm trying to hide it."

Jordan handed out bacon and eggs. The eel, thank God, was nowhere to be seen.

"Your choices are treatment or rest," he said, passing her a plate.

"But resting will add another day to the trip."

Mike didn't look too thrilled, either. "Have the massage," he urged.

Passing out cutlery, Jordan said quietly, "You won't enjoy it, if that's what you're worried about." His blue eyes teased her. "I'm talking therapeutic, not sensual massage."

"I know that," Kate snapped, hating the rush of heat to her cheeks.

She took her plate and sat next to Andrew, who looked as if he'd had the same poor night's sleep she'd had. With his blond hair in tufts, he had the faint indentation of a sleeping bag zipper across his cheek.

Kate realized she hadn't brushed her own hair yet, and touched it experimentally. Oh, God. She flattened it as best she could, caught Jordan hiding a smirk, and turned her back on him to talk to Andrew. "How are you doing this morning?"

"I'm okay, I guess," he said. "And you missed a bit." She felt a tug as he pulled a curl straight.

"Thanks." Kate ignored Jordan's laugh. She stopped trying to cut her bacon—she simply couldn't apply enough pressure—picked it up and bit into it ferociously. Then stopped when she realized everyone was staring at her.

"Okay," she said, "I'll take the massage."

"Hey, Jord," Andrew called, "can I borrow your pebble?"

Dillon, Mike and Kate watched with interest as Jordan felt in the pockets of his pants, then handed over a tiny stone.

"Is it gold?" Dillon asked. Jordan shook his head. "Silver, maybe? A diamond?"

"It's only a pebble, Dil." Andrew pocketed it. "I'll give it back to you later," he said to his uncle.

"What's it for?" Dillon couldn't let the subject rest.

"Andrew will tell you if he wants to," said Jordan.

"I don't," Andrew said, which only made Dillon more desperate to know. He kept pestering until the teenager said, "It's for making decisions, okay?"

Dillon was clearly puzzled. "How does a pebble make a decision?"

"Come closer," said Andrew. Dillon did. "Now listen, very, very hard, and the pebble will speak to you."

"You're fooling."

"Okay." Andrew shrugged. "If you don't want to know the secret…"

Kate watched the child and the adult in Dillon struggle. The child won. "All right, all right." He sat next to Andrew.

"Listen hard…" The teen held the pebble to Dillon's ear. "Are you listening, Dil-boy?"

He nodded, half embarrassed, half entranced. Andrew leaned forward so his mouth was next to the pebble. "You're a very gullible little boy."

Dillon fell on the laughing teenager. "I knew you were tricking…I did," he protested, starting to laugh himself. The two tumbled on the ground and rolled around in a mock fight, which somehow ended up with Jordan holding Andrew down so Dillon could tickle him.

"You can tell they've been doing this for years," Kate commented as, laughing, she and Mike retreated to a safer spot.

"Yeah." His smile was both wistful and bitter as he watched Jordan and his son play the payback game. "How can I compete with that?"

CHAPTER TEN

To HER MORTIFICATION, Kate had to ask for Jordan's help taking off her T-shirt.

"You must really have pushed the pain barrier yesterday if you can't even lift your arms above your head." Gently he slipped the garment off. "You're the last person I'd expect to have a problem speaking up."

Intent on dragging a pillow against her front, Kate didn't bite back. She didn't own sensible underwear—a secret vice she wanted to keep secret. Fortunately, her track pants covered the thong.

Lying facedown on her air bed, she tensed as Jordan expertly undid her bra.

"Relax, Kate, I'm not going to jump you. I said all the running was yours, so unless I get an explicit invitation, you're safe."

"Maybe we should go back to Mr. Slick. I'd forgotten how arrogant you could be…"

This is exactly like being at the physiotherapist's, she told herself, except her therapist didn't make her tremble when he laid his hands on her bare skin. Then the cold salve hit her back, and Kate had an excuse to shiver.

"You know," Jordan said conversationally, "I've been wondering why you haven't mentioned your fiancé in over twenty-four hours. You must be missing him."

"Desperately."

Jordan started working the ointment into her skin. "Now that we're back to being honest with each other, I want to ask you something that's been bothering me. Don't you think it's dishonest accepting one man's proposal when you really want another?"

She tensed. "Don't flatter yourself. And Peter didn't propose, *I* did."

The revelation was supposed to crush him. Instead Jordan laughed delightedly.

"What the hell does *that* mean?" she demanded.

"Nothing." The salve grew warm under the friction of his palms, and Kate thought, *This doesn't hurt.* Then his strong fingers started relentlessly teasing out the knots in her shoulders and upper back. "Don't resist, go with it."

Yeah, right. Biting her lip, she tried to relax into the heat being generated by the firm strokes, but it seemed for every painful muscle that dissolved under Jordan's remorseless ministrations, another, more tender one was uncovered. "Stop," she ground out when she couldn't stand the agony any longer.

Jordan laughed callously. "After I've done your triceps."

If anything, that was worse. She ended up panting and damp with sweat. "You're killing me," she croaked.

"No pain, no gain." Jordan rehooked her bra, then toweled her down as vigorously as if she were a wet dog. "Turn over so I can do your biceps."

Shakily, Kate sat up and turned around. "Look at this," she accused, holding out her trembling arms. "You've crippled me."

"Oh, my God."

Mollified, Kate lowered them. "Remorse is all very well, but how—" Then she saw he was staring at her breasts through her semi-transparent lace bra. Hastily, she crossed her arms.

"Damn it, all that does is accentuate your cleavage." He turned away, adding harshly, "Get dressed."

Kate grabbed her T-shirt and tried to shrug into it, but her muscles were jelly. She kept struggling until, with an oath, Jordan turned back, seized the shirt and started dressing her.

Except, with his eyes averted, she ended up with her head jammed into one of the sleeves. It wasn't a good time for Kate's sense of the ridiculous to kick in. Still, she couldn't choke back her laughter.

If anything, Jordan got angrier, untangling the T-shirt and trying to yank it over her head. "What are you doing, wearing underwear like that on a bush trip? You should be wearing some kind of sports bra."

Beneath the shirt, Kate started laughing in earnest. She ached like a sore tooth, she was light-headed with fatigue, and the incongruity of being scolded by *this* man for wearing sexy underwear struck her as exquisitely funny.

She'd dreaded this massage, convinced it would be a sensual assault. Instead she'd been tortured and pummeled, and now Jordan was acting like an outraged moralist. Her head popped through the neck of the T-shirt.

"Oh, you think this is funny?" He twisted the cotton so it tightened like a straitjacket around her arms, which were still caught inside. But she knew he got the joke. It made him incredibly appealing.

Her urge to kiss him was unexpected

and overwhelming. Jordan saw it and his eyes darkened. She started to struggle and immediately he released her. Breathless, Kate wriggled her arms into the sleeves. "I'm doing the running, right?"

He nodded. She got up and ran.

JORDAN WATCHED KATE. She sat rigidly in front of him, staring straight ahead and paddling like grim death.

The morning air smelled alpine fresh under the ice-blue sky, and the wild beauty of the forest dazzled the eye. But she was oblivious to their surroundings.

Despite being a stickler for the truth, she seemed to have trouble digesting it sometimes. She'd wanted to kiss him and nearly had.

He'd resisted the scrap of lace she called a bra, reminding himself that he had more important priorities now than pursuing a romance with Kate. But then she'd looked at him in a way that jumped all over his common sense.

He'd have blown it if she'd stayed. Completely and utterly blown it.

Jordan put no credence in her sudden engagement. How could he after that incredible kiss? If Kate wanted to kid herself that it was a one-off aberration, that was fine. He knew differently.

But he couldn't convince her otherwise until she'd written a positive article about him and the kids' camp. Then he'd... What?

Kate said curiously over her shoulder, "What's so funny?"

"A pig just flew overhead."

She frowned. "I'm getting tired of people making fun of my fears."

"I'll stop," he promised, because she'd hit their problem bang on. She was scared of their attraction because of her assessment of his character. Change the foundations and everything else would fall into place. *One brick at a time, little piggie,* he reminded himself. *Don't be tempted to shortcut with straw just because a woman tempts you to get the bedroom built.*

The episode in the tent had been a close call—and a timely reminder not to lower his guard just because Kate had agreed to a truce. He wasn't out of the woods yet.

Jordan stopped paddling and checked his river notes. "Over here, everyone," he called, and noticed Mike listened to him now. At least that was one problem solved. They paddled out of the current and beached in the shallows. "We've got our first rapids coming up."

Yahooing, the two boys slapped the water with their paddles.

"Andrew, give Dillon the kayak and go down with Mike…sit at the back and steer."

"What's the grade?" Mike asked. "If it's not high I'd like to try it."

Jordan hesitated, then realized he was doing so only because it was Mike. "You're right, you can handle it. But I want Dillon and Andrew changing places… just in case." The boys tumbled out of the boats.

"In case of what? Capsizing?" Kate's

face was the same dusty chalk as the cliff behind her.

"It won't happen," Jordan reassured her, "I'm only taking precautions because Mike's steering his first white water."

"And you think I'll cock it up." The antagonism was back in Mike's tone.

Jordan realized the problem *wasn't* solved, and pinned the other man with his gaze. "It's not up for negotiation."

Mike broke eye contact first. With bad grace, he shifted forward in the canoe.

Heart pounding, Kate fumbled for her paddle and stared fearfully ahead as Jordan ferried their canoe back out into the current. They drifted around a bend in the river and, sure enough, saw a long stretch of white water heaving and bucking in the distance. She jumped as Jordan's hand tightened reassuringly on her shoulder.

"It's a baby." He shifted back to his seat." Just paddle how and where I tell you, and enjoy the ride."

Kate gripped the paddle harder. Then they hit, and as they tipped and lurched through the flumes of spray, she found herself struggling for balance and trying to follow the rapid-fire instructions coming from behind her. In a brief respite between rapids, she wiped the spray out of her eyes with a shaky hand.

"You're doing great. You're a natural." Jordan's easy assurance soothed her. The next time it was easier, because her terror abated to manageable fear. Two more stretches of rapids, then suddenly—flat water.

Having proved there was life in the old girl yet, the river reverted to a stately promenade through the gorge. The gurgle and hiss of white water died and the sounds of the bush—noisy with the hum of insects—reasserted itself.

Exhausted, Kate slumped forward, but she was aware of a curious exhilaration. The other craft passed them, Andrew and Dillon hooting and hollering, Mike grinning from ear to ear. "We done good, Kate," he yelled, giving her a victory sign.

"Here, have a barley sugar," said Jordan.

Taking the sweet, Kate noticed adrenaline had upped the voltage that powered Jordan's blue eyes. Her pulse, only just beginning to settle down, sped up again, and she finally stopped kidding herself. No matter what her mind told her, her body reacted to Jordan's sexual magnetism as though he was true north.

Strands of wet hair clung to his face and he paused to pull them back into a ponytail. It occurred to Kate that she'd been wrong in one of her assumptions about him. He wasn't vain. In the past twenty-four hours there had been none of the gestures that marked a narcissist. "Why is your hair long?" she asked curiously.

He returned to paddling. "Are you reviewing your 'vanity advised by bad taste' theory?"

"Maybe."

"I wear it long because it annoys people."

"And we know how you like annoying people."

"It annoys a particular sort," he clarified. "The sort that think there's one right way of living and being. Not surprisingly, always theirs. It's also a personal reminder not to judge by appearances."

She ignored the inference. "Were your parents strict?"

"What?" he asked lazily. "Are you going to psychoanalyze me now?"

"I'm a journalist. I ask questions."

"Mum was adamant that all her kids would receive a good education. On Dad's wages, and with five of us, that was quite some mission, so she got a job cleaning at our local college at about the age I started to care what people thought."

There was none of his usual flippancy as he stared out across the river. "For a while I managed to keep out of her way. Then one day she walked into the classroom, mop in hand, with my lunch—I'd forgotten it—and the secret was out." He steered them around a snag.

"Some of the boys gave me a hard time, and I thought they were right to. I even lectured her after school about staying the hell away from me." He looked over at Kate. "I'm still making it up to her."

Jordan suddenly realized he was giving too much away. He dug his paddle into the water and grinned. "And the fact that it ties into a caveman fantasy for women is a bonus." Her lovely mouth tightened in disapproval and he couldn't resist winding her up some more. "But I only use my powers for good," he assured her. "Good times."

Shaking her head, Kate returned to paddling.

"I'm joking," he said, then thought about it. "Well, mostly. C'mon, Kate. Don't tell me you've never once capitalized on your looks."

Water splashed the side of the canoe as she mistimed her stroke. Didn't she know she was gorgeous? Jordan dropped the banter. "What intrigues me most about you are the contrasts." His gaze traveled over her straight back. "On the page you're all passion, Joan of Arc willing to burn for a good cause. But in person you invest a hell of a lot of energy into being Ms. Prim, right down to straightening your red hair."

Automatically, her free hand went to flatten it. "It's brown," she corrected, without looking back. "And I'm *not* passionate. I'm sensible and responsible and careful."

He winced. "Why is *passion* such a bad word for you?"

"Because too often it's used as an excuse for bad behavior. You don't hear about crimes of moderation."

"I think I'm beginning to understand why you're with Peter."

Her back stiffened. "There's a lot to be said for sharing the same worldview."

"Even if it's black-and-white?"

CHAPTER ELEVEN

"TELL ME HOW THE PEBBLE helps make decisions." Dillon figured if he kept pestering Andrew long enough, sooner or later he'd grind him down. It usually worked that way with Mum. But Andrew had younger brothers and sisters, and was proving a harder nut to crack.

"What's it worth?"

"My favorite marble?" Dillon knew it was a long shot, but it was the only treasure that had been small enough to bring on the trip. Andrew just laughed.

"Two bucks," said Mike, who was lying on the grass with his baseball cap pulled over his eyes. They'd stopped for lunch and everyone was taking the chance to rest except Jordan, who'd gone for a walk.

Dillon had thought about going with him, but didn't want to lose ground in his campaign to make Andrew tell.

"Ten dollars," Andrew countered.

Mike snorted. "Dream on."

"Your loss," said Andrew. Dillon's hopes, which had begun to rise, sank again.

Kate put down her book and winked at Dillon. "Five," she said. "Take it or leave it."

"Okay." Andrew shrugged. "But it's not that exciting. Jordan told me he was twenty when his dad died and he had to be the man of the house 'cause he was the oldest and Nana wasn't coping. And he had a heap of things to deal with that he didn't have a clue about."

Andrew tossed the pebble in the air and then caught it again with the same hand.

"When he couldn't decide which decision was the right one, he'd choose according to the pebble in his pocket. He'd read it in some military book when he was a kid…some commander guy did it. If the pebble was smooth side up, decision A. Rough side up, decision B."

The adults seemed to get it; Dillon didn't. "But what if the pebble was wrong?"

"You have two choices," Mike said, "both with equal merits. In the heat of battle, it doesn't matter which one the commander picks, only that he picks one."

"I always watch the air hostess when there's turbulence," Kate said. "As long as she's calm, I'm calm. When you're scared, you want reassurance that the person in charge knows what they're doing. It's like that, Dillon."

He was disappointed. "Andrew was right. That's not very exciting." Secretly, he'd been hoping for magic.

"Not worth five dollars, anyway." Mike pulled the cap back over his eyes.

"I think I got my money's worth," said Kate.

Dillon thought of something and scooted closer to Andrew. "So why do *you* need the pebble?"

Andrew groaned.

"Just tell me," Dillon coaxed, "and I'll go away."

JORDAN CALLED A HALT midafternoon, and this time, no one argued. They were all weary. "How about a bush walk," he suggested after they'd made camp. "It will loosen up sore muscles, and there's a neat site only a forty-minute hike from here."

To his surprise, Mike accepted. "I need to stretch my legs."

Andrew took more persuading. He was back to brooding, which meant the pebble hadn't told him what he wanted to hear.

Last week he'd had a fight with his girl-friend, which had escalated into a breakup. It was Megan's fault, he'd told Jordan, all outraged teen male. Andrew had accepted the river trip, then discovered it conflicted with Megan's high-school dance at her private girls' college.

It had just gone downhill from there.

Jordan liked Megan and had always

thought his nephew took advantage of her conciliatory nature, but Andrew's misery took away any pleasure in saying I told you so. Instead, Jordan had come up with a suggestion, which Andy was agonizing over. In the teenager's eyes, it meant backing down. In his uncle's, it meant growing up. It would be interesting to see what his nephew chose to do.

In the meantime, everyone suffered. For the third time, Andy changed his mind about coming on the hike. "It'll be boring."

"You know what?" Enough was enough. "Stay in camp…you're cooking dinner."

Howls of protest followed them into the bush.

"And I want it made with love," Jordan yelled back. "That's what my mother used to say to me," he confided to Dillon, who was walking beside him. "Cooking dinner was always her punishment when I misbehaved."

"Is that why you're so good at it?" Dillon asked.

Kate and Mike burst out laughing.

"You know," said Jordan. "I believe it is."

The river disappeared as they followed the track through dense forest into a narrow valley hemmed in by steep bluffs, where green mosses, creepers and ferns colonized the ancient trees.

It was like walking through prehistory until they came upon a solid concrete bridge spanning a deep gorge. Jordan stepped aside to enjoy everyone's reaction. Kate stopped abruptly and checked behind her, possibly to confirm the rough track was still there. Mike looked ahead, beyond the bridge, to where the forest closed in again. Dillon said, "Cool," ran straight onto it and jumped up and down to test its stability.

"It's okay," Jordan said, when Mike started forward. "It's safe."

"What is it?"

"The Bridge to Nowhere."

They all followed Dillon onto the high span and leaned over the concrete balustrade.

"I've read about it," said Mike. "After World War I the government gave returning servicemen plots of land here, and the chance to carve a new future out of the wilderness. Come look, Kate."

Jordan found a stand of exotic trees, all that remained of one former homestead. "Heartbreak allotments, they were called. Prone to erosion. Cut off from the outside world, the homesteaders struggled to make a living in the middle of the Depression."

He ran his hands over the rough surface, rutted by age.

"Most of them walked off the land in the end, but not before the government built this bridge to service the valley. The bush reclaimed the road, and now the bridge is all that's left of those farmers' hopes and dreams—a novelty for hikers."

"You know a lot about this place," Kate said curiously.

"My grandparents were one of the few families that stayed. My mother grew up around here."

Mike gave a short laugh. "So bloody-mindedness is a family trait?"

"We Kings prefer the word *resolute*." Jordan smoothed a couple of stray hairs back out of his eyes. "But you're right. Telling us something is impossible is like waving a red rag at a bull." His gaze gravitated to Kate. When he looked back, Mike was watching him.

"Interesting," said Mike, and Jordan knew he wasn't talking about his story.

"This would be a great place for shooting practice," Dillon said, running toward them. "You could set up cans on the ledge. They'd fall miles."

"And then you'd have to try to find them," said Kate. "You can't leave litter here."

"What do you know about guns, son?" Mike asked.

"Jordan and I do target practice…and when I'm fourteen you're going to buy me a gun, aren't you, Jord?"

"Oh no, he's not," Mike growled.

"An air gun," Jordan reassured him, "to

be kept at my house and used under supervision."

"No son of mine will own a gun."

"Claire has no problem with it," Jordan said pointedly.

A tide of red swept up the other man's face. "I don't care, it's not on."

"Dad, please," Dillon begged. "I'm really careful. Jordan's taught—"

Mike lost his temper. "I don't give a damn what Jordan's taught you or what Jordan thinks. I'm your father and *I* say no guns."

Dillon's lower lip jutted out, and unconsciously, he moved closer to Jordan. "We'll sort it out with your mother, mate," Jordan murmured, ruffling the boy's hair.

"Don't try and undermine my authority, King." Mike's voice had become dangerously quiet.

Jordan snorted. "Excuse me if I find it hard to muster respect, Mike. You haven't been around for eleven years."

"Stop it," Kate said. "You're upsetting Dillon."

Both men ignored her. "Claire's family kept me out," said Mike.

"And you accepted it," Jordan sneered. "You see, that's the difference between us. I wouldn't have."

"I haven't got your wealth, your influence."

"If I was as poor as dirt I'd never relinquish my child."

"Don't you push me!" yelled Mike. "Not if you want to stay in Dillon's life."

Jordan laughed scornfully. "Empty threats from a hollow man."

"Stop it, both of you!" Kate cradled Dillon, who was covering his ears.

"Aww, no, Dil-boy." Jordan started forward at the same time as Mike. The two stopped and glared at each other.

Kate led Dillon away from them. "You're standing on the Bridge to Nowhere and you still don't get it. This is a *child,* not a bone to fight over, and there can never be too many people who love him. Come on, darling, let's leave them to it."

"Shit," said Jordan, after they'd gone. "Shit, shit!" He kicked at the concrete balustrade, furious at Mike, more furious at himself. "Why the hell did you come on this trip?" he demanded. "Why, when you hate me so much?"

"Because Claire and I are talking of re-marrying," Mike snapped. "And she wanted us to bond, for Dillon's sake." Seeing Jordan's shock, he added, "So don't tell *me* I don't have any power."

"I HATE MY DAD."

Alternatively sobbing and grinding his teeth, Dillon walked back to camp with Kate.

"Don't say that," she said. "You don't mean it."

"He keeps fighting with Jordan, and now he says I can't have a gun." Dillon's chest heaved and he let loose another outburst of sobbing.

"Oh, Dillon." She stopped and hugged him, and because they were alone, he let her.

"It's only because Jordan wants to give it to me, that's the only reason."

"Jordan is just as much to blame as your dad is." Kate sounded mad, too. "He shouldn't have said he'd only listen to your mum. You wouldn't like it, would you, if your opinion got ignored?"

But Jordan was perfect. "Dad's been fighting with Jord the whole time," he said. "It's all his fault. I hate him."

"I don't want to hear you say that again," Kate reprimanded.

"You hate *your* dad."

Her eyes widened in shock. "I *never* said that."

"Why else wouldn't you see him then?" In one of their many chats, Dillon had discovered Kate hadn't seen her father for seven years. When he'd asked why, she'd refused to talk about it.

She got flustered. "He lives in another country."

"Do you talk to him on the phone?"

She struggled to answer, and Dillon

recalled his own troubles. "The only thing I want in the whole world is a gun," he whined, ignoring the fact that his birthday list was two pages long.

"Well, you can't have it." Looking behind him, Dillon saw Mike striding to catch up to them. For a moment he worried that his dad had heard him say he hated him. Then he stuck out his lower lip. Mike looked at Kate. "Mind falling behind?"

"Sure." She stopped and settled by the side of the path. When the boy opened his mouth to protest, she cut him off. "Go with your dad, Dillon."

Dillon stormed ahead. Well, he wasn't going to talk to Mike, no way. For ten minutes they marched through the bush without speaking, while Dillon tried to leave his father behind. Mike started puffing, but kept up. The boy's pace slowed as the anger worked its way through his system, until all that was left were bewilderment and sadness. He finally blinked away tears.

"When you're ready to talk, I'll tell you a secret," Mike said from behind him.

Dillon's interest was captured, but he feigned disinterest for another fifty yards. "What?" he grunted, slowing somewhat.

Mike finally reached him and they walked side by side. "If I tell you, you must promise not to tell anyone, Dillon. The only other person who knows is your mother."

There was such gravity in his father's tone that Dillon shivered. "Okay."

"I had a brother," Mike said. "His name was Dave. He was a year older than me, and we were best friends. He and Dad used to love to go hunting, but I always tried to get out of it. I was a hopeless shot and I much preferred staying at home painting my model airplane."

"You see, Dad, you're just saying I can't because *you* don't like it."

Mike put a hand on Dillon's shoulder and they kept walking. "But this one time my dad made me go…I'd turned fourteen and he thought I should be doing more manly things, I guess. I was pretty sulky about it, and eventually he got mad and told me to go back to the car. I got bored, so while I was waiting for them I started shooting at trees. Stupid, thoughtless kids' stuff. Except they were coming back…"

Mike's footsteps had slowed until they were barely moving, and suddenly Dillon wanted his dad to stop talking. He knew how this story was going to end, and maybe if Dillon interrupted before Dad said it, somehow it could end differently. But he couldn't say a word, not even when Mike's fingers dug painfully into his shoulder.

"I shot my brother and he died. That's why I can't let you have a gun, son."

CHAPTER TWELVE

"YOU KNOW WHAT YOUR problem is?" Kate barely waited until Jordan was within earshot.

"Don't," he interrupted wearily. "I can't handle a lecture right now."

"Empathy," she continued. "You're a big, good-looking man with wealth and power, and you can't relate to ordinary people's insecurities."

"You've been practicing this, haven't you?"

But she wasn't listening. "Most men are weaker than you, Jordan. They shouldn't be despised for it. If Mike got pushed out of Dillon's life by Claire's family, he should be pitied. You accuse me of being judgmental. Well, I haven't got a patch on you. And as for making Dillon listen to it…"

Jordan flinched. "You don't have to hit me over the head with that one. I've been doing that myself."

"He's very upset." Seeing the torment on Jordan's face, Kate relented. "Don't worry, Mike's sorting it out." Jordan still looked desperate, so she added, "And I'm sure he'll apologize for you."

That won a weak smile. "Cheering up people is not one of your talents, is it?"

"That depends on whether you think you've suffered enough."

"No," he said, "but looks like I'm going to. Mike said he and Claire are considering remarrying, and he's made it clear he's going to try to influence my access to Dillon."

"Then it's even more important that you apologize to him."

Jordan deliberately misunderstood her. "Dillon? I intend to."

"I'm talking about Mike."

"Well, it's been lovely chatting," he said. "We really must do it again. But I'm leaving now before I say something that might negatively influence your decision about my fitness as camp trustee." To Kate's annoyance he left the path and disappeared into the bush.

"An apology to Mike might swing it for you," she called after him, but Jordan didn't answer. He probably knew she didn't mean it.

Oddly, her opinion *was* beginning to change. He was still the arrogant man he'd always been, but Andrew's story about the pebble indicated Jordan had a vulnerable side. He just never showed it to her. Or Mike. She sighed. Every time he looked as if he was going to redeem himself, he did something stupid.

It was very quiet, standing alone in the forest, with only the faint rustle of leaves and the occasional birdsong. Kate hadn't been truly alone for days, and was enjoying her solitary walk back to camp when she heard something snap close to her. Too close.

She ran the rest of the way.

"WE'VE EATEN, done dishes, cleaned ourselves up and it's only seven o'clock. What do we do now?"

Jordan took a minute to answer Mike, figuring he'd only get himself into trouble. The two men had managed to get through the evening by exchanging the barest civilities. Jordan bitterly regretted losing his temper in front of the kid, but otherwise he was unrepentant. He turned to face Mike and said mildly enough, "A sing-along beside the campfire?"

"Games it is," said Mike. "Dillon, you choose."

"I don't mind."

Jordan frowned. He and Dillon were back on good terms and Dillon and Mike seemed okay, too. Still, the boy seemed distracted. When Jordan had found a quiet moment to tell him not to give up on the gun until

Jordan talked to Claire, Dillon had said he'd changed his mind and didn't want it.

"How about cards," suggested Andrew. Another kid who needed cheering up.

"Poker, high stakes," said Jordan, because it was his nephew's favorite game. Jordan had supplemented his university scholarship playing poker before Christian and Luke had press-ganged him into the more legitimate business that had started their empire. Andy had learned most of his tricks.

Andrew brightened. "Cash?"

"The loser makes hot chocolate."

"I'm in," said Kate.

Now that was interesting, Jordan thought. This woman wasn't a risk taker, so she must be good.

"Not my game," said Mike. "Dillon, you want to take the rods down to the river for some night fishing?"

Dillon instantly perked up. "Would I!"

Kate did prove to be a good card player, but Jordan was still surprised by just how good she was. "Where does a nice convent girl learn tricks like that?" he asked, after she'd changed her play for a third time to stop him and Andrew from getting a fix on her.

"My father taught me." There was a repressive note in her voice telling him to back off.

Jordan loved No Trespassing signs. "Tell us about him," he invited.

"He never talks when he's playing cards," she said.

Amused, Jordan dropped the subject, and the three of them got down to business.

Andrew ended up making the drinks, which he did with a good-natured complaint. "I'm supposed to be the hustler here."

While they waited for their hot chocolate, Jordan reshuffled the deck. "Another couple of hands?" It was difficult to keep count of the cards when the firelight danced in her hair and flushed her cheeks. But it was her eyes that made his throat go dry—flashing challenges, sparking with laughter when she teased him with her wins.

Playing back to a draw, he took her on the last hand.

"When am I going to learn," she said, "that that guileless look of yours means trouble?" Dillon and Mike came back from the river and she nodded to them. "How'd it go?"

"Lots of bites. No fish."

"That's because all the sharks are here," said Kate. "What's your favorite game, Dillon? Let's play that."

He and Mike joined the circle. "Truth or dare."

Jordan didn't think Kate would like that. But he saw only a flicker of dismay before she rallied. "Great idea."

What was it about this woman? So self-righteous, so kind, so provocative, so prim. *When this is over and the future of the kids' camp is secure, you and I, Ms. Brogan, are going to sort out this attraction once and for all.*

"Lemme go first, lemme go first." Dillon pointed to Andrew.

"Truth," said Andrew.

"What decision do you have to make?" asked Dillon gleefully.

Andrew blushed and looked at Jordan. "I don't have to answer that, do I?"

"You can always forfeit…. What's your price, Dillon?"

"He could carry me around on his back for the rest of the night."

"Okay, okay," said Andrew. "I'm trying to decide whether to call my girlfriend and apologize. We broke up before the trip and it was kinda my fault."

"But you can't phone her, can you?" asked Kate. "We're not in range."

"Actually, we're in that hot spot I told you about," Jordan said.

"And you didn't tell me…. My God, I could have been working…." She scrambled to her feet, saw Dillon's look of disappointment and sat down again. "After the game."

"And the pebble didn't help?" Mike asked Andrew.

Jordan started. "How do you know about that?"

"They all do," said Andrew. "Kate gave me five bucks to tell them. I knew you wouldn't mind."

Did he? Before Jordan could decide, a disgusted Dillon flung himself on his back. "Man, I should've chosen dare."

"What did the pebble say, Andrew?" asked Kate.

"Not to call," he mumbled miserably.

Jordan grinned. "Andy, if I disagreed with the pebble's judgment, I overrode it. It was only there to prompt a decision."

"You never told me *that* part."

"Well, now I have." Jordan relaxed against his log backrest. "What are you going to do?"

Andrew didn't answer. He just pulled out his cell phone and ran for the trees.

"I'm *never* gonna be that silly over a girl," said Dillon. "Okay, whose turn is it?"

"Mine," said Kate. "I dare your dad and Jordan to spend five minutes in pleasant conversation."

Both men groaned. Dillon giggled nervously.

"I'll make it easy for you," she said, "by feeding you questions. Jordan, ask Mike to tell you about his childhood. I'm sure it's not that different from yours."

Jordan looked at Mike. For once they were in complete agreement with each other. "Forfeit," they said simultaneously.

Kate looked at Dillon. "Can they do that?"

He nodded, disappointment on his small face, then he whispered in her ear. Her lips curved in a smile. "Or you can share a tent tonight," she said.

"Well, Jordan," said Mike, setting his watch. "Where would you like me to start?"

"Brothers or sisters?"

Dillon gasped, drawing Jordan's attention. Mike said quietly, "Only child."

No wonder you're bloody hopeless at sharing. "Your parents live where?"

"Apart. They separated when I was fifteen when my…" he paused "…when Mum and I moved to Scottsdale." Jordan knew it. The guy came from a tiny southern town with big social problems, best known for the pervasive stink of its slaughterhouse.

Jordan was curious now. "How did you meet Claire?"

"She was spending summer holidays with farming relatives…and was the only other person using the library."

Andrew returned, obviously in high spirits. "We're back together and Megan's not taking anyone else to the dance. She only said it to make me jealous." His face creased in a sheepish grin. "Man, did *that* work." He plunked himself down by the fire. "I wish I could make it up to her by being back for it tomorrow night, but she said she knows we can't get home till Monday." His tone was both wistful and resigned.

Jordan took pity on him. "Why don't I arrange for a jetboat to come upriver and pick you up tomorrow? You could be back in Auckland by late afternoon."

Kate looked at him in surprise. "Why, Jordan, you're a romantic."

"Take that back," he said.

"But—but that would be expensive, wouldn't it?" Andrew stammered. "I mean, wouldn't it? And I've been such a dork."

Jordan laughed. "Is that a yes?"

"Yes!" His nephew fell on him with a bear hug. Jordan broke free and massaged his ribs. "And watch the hair," he said, "I just washed it tonight." He caught sight of Kate's slight frown. "Truth," he said, "for Kate. Why does my long hair annoy you so much?"

"It's still my turn," she reminded him sweetly. "You and Mike have only had two minutes of pleasant conversation."

"Hey, I'm happy to wait," said Mike. "Besides, I've got a feeling this will be good."

"You won't like it," she warned Jordan, "and I feel mean saying it, now that I know why you…"

"C'mon, Kate, don't go soft on me now."

"To *me,* it seems like a demand for attention that reflects a certain immaturity. To *me,*" she stressed again.

"You read it as a sign I can't grow up?" Jordan said incredulously.

"It's a personal view," she said. "And you did ask."

"I did," he conceded. "I won't tell you what I read into your own regimented shortcut."

She bristled. "I've been told it's very chic."

"People are just being polite."

"Something no one could accuse you of."

"I like it now, though," he said, "all wild red curls."

"Brown." She flattened them. "My hair is brown."

"No, it's not," said Dillon, clearly puzzled. "Is it my turn again yet?" He was happy once more, Jordan realized. *Bless you, Kate.*

"No," said Andrew. "It's mine, and it's payback, kid." He stroked his chin, covered with light down after two days in the wilds, and thought hard. "Jump in the river tomorrow."

"That's it?" Andrew was infamous for his dares.

"I know," Andrew said regretfully, "but I'm too happy to think nasty, though I have a great one for Kate. Go into the forest and call, "'Piggie, piggie, pig.'"

"That's not scary," she bluffed.

"And wait five minutes for an answer," Andrew added.

"I liked you better when you were sad," she said, getting up with great dignity.

"You don't want to forfeit?" Jordan said in surprise. He knew her fear was real.

"The awful thing about being the only girl on this trip," she replied, "is that you can't let your side down."

She disappeared into the bush and they

heard her quavering voice calling for pigs. The boys started to giggle and snort. Andrew said, "Dil-boy, let's go scare her." Jordan and Mike grabbed a boy each.

"She's got enough on her plate," said Mike, looking at Jordan, who frowned. *What the hell was that supposed to mean?*

Kate reappeared five minutes later, trembling, white as milk, but with a big, cheesy grin on her face. Jordan led the cheers, a curious tightness in his chest.

"Okay," she said, when everything had settled down. "That deserves an extra turn, and I thought of something I want to know when I was waiting in the forest. Jordan—" he smiled at her "—why do you think my fiancé's an…" She glanced at Dillon and started again. "In my office last week you started to tell me something about Peter, and stopped. What was it?"

Jordan stopped smiling. "Forfeit."

"No," she said, her gaze very steady. "Tell me."

"He came to see me on the day of the

party," Jordan finally said. "To apologize for your bad judgment in writing that column."

"I don't believe you," she responded, almost mechanically. Jordan watched the blood drain from her face. "He's never enjoyed my writing, but…"

She stopped, staring at him in bewilderment, and he wanted to leave it there, painfully aware that his own needs—not hers—had driven him to give her the truth so brutally. But too much was at stake now, and not only the camp. "I don't want you to marry the wrong guy."

Kate clasped a hand to her heart and said lightly, "I had no idea *your* proposal was so serious."

"You know what I mean…. You deserve better."

The air seemed suddenly chilly; she hugged herself. "Whose turn is it?"

The others were silent.

"You can't still mean to marry him," Jordan said impatiently.

"We've been together a long time."

"Well, if he's so damn right for you, Kate, then why didn't you get married years ago?"

"We were waiting until my younger brother and sister left home."

"Didn't Peter want to help you raise them?"

"They were my responsibility, not his."

"Really? I thought marriage was a partnership." When Kate didn't answer, Jordan said slowly, "They don't like him, do they?"

"Mike—" desperately, Kate glanced to her left "—your turn, I think."

But Jordan wouldn't let it go. "Some types of security come at too high a cost, Kate."

"Says the man who's never needed it," she retorted. "Not all of us see marriage as the bogeyman, Jordan."

"Hear, hear," said Mike.

"Maybe I never met the right woman," Jordan said.

"Maybe you were never the right man," Mike countered.

"What the hell's that supposed to mean? And butt out."

"Because you don't get hurt," Kate answered, "you forget that you can hurt other people." Her voice caught. "For instance, this Mr. Up Front bull you spin about dating. Do you think if a woman has feelings for you, she's going to walk away? No, she's going to stick around and try to change your mind. And suffer when you move on. You're smart enough to know that."

"Not everyone falls in love with me."

"Mum did," Dillon said.

Kate became aware of her surroundings. Dillon was looking fascinated, Mike tight-lipped and Andrew hugely embarrassed. "Oh, God," she said. "I'm so sorry." Mortified, she scrambled to her feet. "I'm calling it a night." Without waiting, she headed for her tent, grabbed her toiletry bag and fled to the river. But when she got there, she just stood in the dark and cried.

Peter had gone behind her back to Jordan with a groveling apology. Kate was suddenly fiercely glad she'd broken off their engagement.

Cleaning her teeth, she admitted an unpalatable truth. Peter had fooled her precisely because he was so different from her father. Actually, she'd fooled herself. She'd been unable to believe that a man who lived by the book and followed social conventions wasn't a good man.

"Kate."

She dipped her flannel in the icy water and scrubbed her face. "Go away, Jordan."

He came closer. "Sometimes people do the wrong thing thinking it's the right thing."

She had no idea if he was apologizing for Peter or himself. She chose the latter, because she had no emotional stake in it. "Like you believing a married woman was single?"

"Or you being spooked by a kiss into getting engaged to the wrong man. Don't marry him, Kate."

"I don't shed lovers as easily as you do. Men like you make me sick."

"You don't have any idea what kind of man I am," he snapped. "You have some sort of crazy template in your head and you keep trying to squeeze me into it." Jordan came closer until he towered over her. "Well, I don't fit, Kate, so let me out of the box or I'll blast the damn thing open."

"You can't make me do anything I don't want to."

He narrowed his eyes. "Can't I?" he said softly. "Can't I really, Kate?" His gaze swept her body, lingering with deliberate provocation.

Under her T-shirt, Kate's nipples jumped to attention. She crossed her arms. "Don't you get it? It doesn't *matter* that I find you physically attractive. I would never disrupt my life for a handsome face and a bad boy's magnetism. You're just like—" She stopped, biting her lower lip.

Jordan's expression was suddenly intent. "Like who?"

"Forget it." She grabbed her toiletries, and the soap fell into the water with a splash.

Jordan retrieved it. "It's obviously not Peter," he mused. "He prefers the underhanded approach."

"I said forget it." Kate hurried back up the path. Jordan lengthened his stride to keep up with her. "So it must be some other guy. But you two have been dating for years."

"Didn't you hear what I said?" She was nearly running now. Her foot caught on a root and she tripped.

Jordan saved her from falling. "I remind you of your father?" he asked incredulously. "Trust me, Kate, I'm nothing like him."

"How would you know?" She stiffened, suddenly suspicious. "You had me investigated, didn't you?"

"Of course I did—you know what's at

stake here. I need to know everything I can about you."

"You're probably coming on to me as another ploy." She'd said that before, and it had made him back off. Worth trying again.

"I can't fake this," he said, and in the dark he kissed her. Kate hadn't been expecting it and she didn't have any defense against the wave of feelings that flooded her senses. Lust, longing…belonging.

Shaken, she shoved him away. "The fact that I'm engaged to Peter doesn't mean anything to you, and yet you ask me to believe you respect the sanctity of marriage."

"Our situation's different, and getting engaged to Peter was your sin, not mine. You know you have feelings for me, so do the right thing and put the poor bastard out of his misery."

The arrogance, the assumptions, the *accuracy* behind his comments took Kate's breath away. "Well, it's been lovely chatting," she managed to choke out at last. "We really must do it again. But I'm leaving now before I kill you."

CHAPTER THIRTEEN

"THERE'LL BE ROOM for one more in the jetboat. Anyone else want to go home?"

Kate saw Jordan was looking at Mike. It was 2:00 p.m., and after six hours paddling they were pitching a new camp, while Jordan walked an excited Andrew down to the rendezvous point.

"Pick me," she said, and meant it.

"You're not going anywhere." Jordan didn't even glance her way. "Mike? The jetboat can tow either the canoe or the kayak."

Mike hesitated, glancing uncertainly at Dillon, and Kate intervened. For Dillon's sake the two men needed to sort out their differences. "All for one and one for all, right, Mike?"

She took Jordan aside. "I'd say conflict resolution was an essential skill for camp trustees, wouldn't you?"

Jordan went up to Mike. "Just joking, mate. Couldn't do it without you."

"Don't patronize me."

Looking back at Kate, Jordan shook his head, as if to say, *It's hopeless.* "Okay, Cinderella," he said to Andrew, "let's get you to the ball." Not only had Jordan arranged a jetboat, he'd also arranged a helicopter to fly his nephew back to Auckland, so Andrew accepted the comparison with good grace.

"See ya, Kate." Blushing slightly, he hugged her, then shook Mike's hand and mussed Dillon's hair. "Bye, squirt."

He headed off down the track with his uncle, then hesitated and ran back. "He is my hero," he reminded Kate earnestly.

"Well, he would say that," Mike commented as they gave Andrew a last wave goodbye, and the two disappeared from sight. "Jetboat, helicopter…that would buy my hero worship, too."

"Well, *you* would say *that*." Kate turned back to the half-pitched tent and started laying out guy ropes. "You dislike him."

Mike hammered in pegs. "Don't you?"

"He drives me crazy, but that doesn't blind me to the fact that he cares about kids. I'm not on anyone's side, Mike, except Dillon's. You need to separate your dislike for Jordan from what's best for your son. Both of you do."

Mike's expression darkened, but before he could say anything Dillon came running over with her cell phone. Too much had been going on last night for Kate to make the calls she wanted to, and he'd spent the time since they'd moored trying to find a signal—after she'd suggested the hot spot might still be warm. Mike had gone into the technical reasons why that was unlikely, but she'd captured Dillon's imagination.

"I even climbed up a tree," he said glumly, "but no signal." That explained the pine needles in his hair.

Kate brushed them off. "Thanks for trying, Dil." She was desperate to know how her brother's dinner with their father had gone.

Dillon saw her disappointment. "Did you want to call your mum?" He'd phoned his last night, fortunately their talk centering on the big eel he'd caught rather than Mike and Jordan's fight.

"My mum's dead. It's okay," Kate added quickly, when he looked alarmed. "It happened a long, long time ago." As though she didn't still ache sometimes with missing her.

"If you're homesick you could call your dad," he suggested. "Oh, I forgot you don't talk to him."

Kate had to laugh. "Go find another tree to climb."

Obligingly, he ran off.

She glanced at Mike. "That made me sound like a terrible daughter…but there are good reasons for our estrangement."

"Knowing you, Kate, I'm sure there are."

They went back to pitching the tent. "There was a 'but' in that statement," she said after a few minutes. "It's bothering me."

Mike put down the hammer. "But… speaking as someone who never repaired a relationship with his father before the man died, I'd say keep trying."

She tried to suppress her exasperation. "It wasn't a fight over using the car, Mike."

"Neither was ours. We let grief push us apart… blame and guilt. But now that he's dead, I wish I'd tried harder to find a way back to him."

His pain, she realized, was as deep as hers. "Sometimes," she said at last, "stepping back seems the only way to save your life…the only way to heal."

"For a time," he agreed, "not forever. I know it sounds corny, but rifts with family…they're not good for your soul."

"Look at me!" Dillon yelled from the top of a totara, his flushed face a rosy berry in the green canopy. They made admiring noises and, satisfied, he started climbing down.

Mike picked up the hammer again and pounded the last peg home. "And I believe in giving people second chances because Claire gave me one with Dillon. I don't know why she changed her mind, but I thank God every day that she did. And this time, I'm going to make it work." He glanced at Kate, who was collecting the superfluous pegs. "I guess you're wondering why I haven't been around for him."

"You don't need to give me an explanation, Mike," she said quietly, retying the tent bag. "I'm not judging you."

"I want to tell you," he said. They both paused in their work. "We were only eighteen and students when Claire got pregnant with Dillon. It was a summer romance with a kid from the wrong side of the tracks. Her parents didn't want us to get married, but we did, so they cut off financial support, hoping the pressure would split us up. It did."

Absently, he started tapping his palm with the hammer. "I wasn't giving myself any breaks at that point in my life so…as far as I was concerned, the separation only proved I wasn't worth much. Jordan was right, I did walk away. I believed it was best for Dillon."

"I'm really happy you're a family again."

"Now *I* can hear a 'but,'" he said, smiling.

"But my dad and I…we're not likely to resolve our differences."

"It must have been pretty bad, Kate."

"I'm starving," Dillon declared. The interruption saved her from having to answer.

She looked at her watch. "I'm not surprised, it's way past lunchtime. I wonder why Jordan's taking so long."

"We don't need him to feed us, do we?" Mike said impatiently. "How about we do a chip fry-up? I know we've got potatoes."

Kate's mouth started to water. "Sure, but I don't know how to assemble the stove."

"Neither do I," said Mike, "but how hard can it be?"

Fifteen minutes later they were almost ready to cook. Sustained by a slab of fruit loaf they'd found in one of the storage bins, Mike and Dillon had peeled and chipped the potatoes, while Kate made a salad of cucumber and tomatoes. "No one's going to eat it," Dillon had pointed out, but she'd told him he'd get scurvy, which had led to a fascinating discussion of other horrible diseases. No one's appetite was the least affected, which just went to show, thought Kate cheerfully, that she'd been spending too much time with little boys.

She dug around in the food barrel, hoping to find salad dressing, but the only bottle she could find held brandy... probably for medicinal purposes. Salt and pepper would have to do. Now for the hard bit. Crouching back on her heels, Kate examined the metal pieces of the portable stove, sniffing the fuel for clues. Then she nearly toppled over as fumes of methylated spirits hit the back of her throat.

"Let me," said Mike with male superiority, and then proceeded to take ten minutes to assemble the stove. With Kate's help.

"Okay, guys, it's showtime." Tentatively, Kate stretched a lit match toward the burner. It went out.

"You need to get closer," said Mike, and she handed him the matches.

"Go ahead."

Twice he tried; twice the wind extinguished it. Mike cursed.

"Maybe we should wait for Jordan," Kate suggested.

Everyone looked at the potatoes, which were starting to discolor.

"I have an idea," said Mike. He repositioned the stove under the canopy that sheltered the tent's entrance, and they all huddled over it, using their bodies as a windbreak. The next match flared and caught.

A wave of fierce heat slammed Kate's face and, with a startled cry, she flung herself backward. So did Dillon and Mike. Dillon's foot knocked the stove against the tent, splattering fuel.

Blue flame licked tentatively at the tent flap, and Mike dived forward, fumbling with the wheel adjuster to turn off the fire, then kicking the apparatus into the clearing.

But it was too late.

JORDAN ADDED ANOTHER fallen branch to the bundle in his arms and paused to absorb the sights and sounds of the bush.

Two fantails flitting nearby squeaked and fussed. They'd been dining on insects disturbed by his footfalls.

Smiling, he turned toward camp and caught a sudden movement out of the corner of his eye. A Captain Cook razor-back boar, about 150 pounds, stood frozen by a rata tree, heaving flanks evidence of its fright. "I wish Kate could see you," he said aloud, and the animal jumped again.

"Scaredy-pig." Jordan turned his back on it and nearly stumbled over a piglet. With a terrified squeal, it vanished like a black streak into the undergrowth. He could barely make out the rear end of a full-grown razorback before they both vanished. Behind him, he heard a heavy grunt, then the thud of hooves.

"You've gotta be kidding me." He spun around to see the boar charging toward him, and flung himself to the left, sending the firewood in all directions. The pig skittered on its hind legs as it turned midrun, then hurtled back, charging again.

Seizing one of the dropped branches, Jordan slammed it across the bristly black hide, twisting away from the sharp tusks as the boar tried to gore and bite him. Still more surprised than afraid, he whacked the pig again, and this time connected with its snout. With a squeal of outrage, the animal tore off through the trees, splintering undergrowth as it went.

As the sound faded, Jordan became

aware of his own heavy breathing, and stumbled back against a tree, sliding to the ground. His first thought was that Kate must never know about this. His second was thank God she'd told him not to run. It had been his first impulse.

He started to laugh until he caught sight of his right thigh. Blood oozed through a slash in his jeans. Examining the wound, he was relieved to see it was shallow. Nothing his first aid kit couldn't handle, and he carried a tetanus shot as part of his medical supplies. At that thought he started to sweat.

But first things first. He pushed himself to his feet and took off his Swanndri, tying it around his waist to conceal his injury. Gathering the scattered wood, he staggered back to camp. Everyone must be wondering where the hell he was.

Jordan smelled the smoke first. Great, they'd got the fire started. Then, through a gap in the forest canopy, he saw a billow of black smoke, large and ominous.

He dropped the wood and ran.

CHAPTER FOURTEEN

SIPPING HER TEA, Kate grimaced at its necessary sweetness, and cast an apprehensive look at Jordan. He stood in stony silence amid the charred debris that had been her tent, toying with the handle of his shovel.

Probably contemplating using it on our heads. She inched farther up the mound where she sat with her codefendants, also wrapped in blankets and holding hot drinks. Adding to their misery, it had been raining for the past half hour. Although now the sun beamed into the clearing through the dispersing cloud.

Lighting up the scene of the crime, she thought despairingly. Jordan lifted the shovel and thumped it into the dirt with a single, powerful thrust. It quivered with the impact, and Kate pulled her knees up to her chin, trying to make herself as unobtrusive as possible. Everybody waited meekly for Jordan's recriminations.

He removed his T-shirt, muscles rippling across his back as he lifted it over his head and dropped it. Kate shivered. Effortlessly, he pulled the shovel out of the ground and started covering the mess with earth.

He'd said nothing for forty minutes, ever since he'd returned to find them flapping at the fire with a flaming blanket. After one pithy expletive, he'd extinguished the flames with a competency that mocked their previous efforts.

Then he'd made everyone sit down, had brewed tea and silently restored the camp to order. Except for a brusque, "Anyone hurt?"

Thank God, no one was.

Just Kate's wardrobe, now being given a decent burial. The only item that had escaped was her wet suit, drying on a tree branch. She had nothing to wear but what she had on. She hoped Jordan would think that punishment enough.

His expression, when she caught glimpses of his face, looked ominous, but her attention kept returning to his half-naked body, perfect in its symmetry and fluidity of movement. Even in a crisis, her feelings were complicated by lust.

Jordan finished his work and turned to face them. "Right," he said, "who's to blame?"

NEVER IN HIS LIFE had Dillon been scared of Jordan. But he was scared now.

Bravely he lifted his chin. "I am," he said. "I knocked it over."

"It's not your fault, son," his dad said quietly. "It was mine. I lit the stove near the tent."

"Our fault," Kate corrected, reaching across Dillon to touch Mike's arm. "The danger didn't occur to me, either."

But Jordan was only looking at Dillon's

dad. "I might have guessed," he said. Jordan was going to kill Mike.

But he didn't. At least, not with his hands. He did it with words. Hard words that Dillon didn't always understand, but felt every time his father flinched beside him.

And Dillon's empty stomach began to hurt as though he'd eaten too much.

Kate kept trying to interrupt, to share some of the blame, but Jordan wouldn't listen. And Dad said nothing, not a word in his own defense, though it really was Dillon's fault for kicking over the stove. If he hadn't kicked it over this wouldn't have happened.

Jordan looked at the surrounding forest, and got even madder. "Do you have any idea what would have happened if the bush had been dry? You could have killed your son and Kate as well as yourself. But then, of course, irresponsibility is part of your nature, isn't it, Mike?"

Dad got smaller and smaller beside him. Dillon could feel him shrinking, and knew Mike was sorry his son was hearing all the terrible things Jordan was saying.

Jordan was wrong. He was in the wrong. The shock made Dillon blink for a minute, then he was on his feet and screaming. "Stop it, Jordan, *stop it!* It's not all Dad's fault, it's mine and Kate's, as well. Stop being a bully."

Jordan shut up. For a moment he and Dillon stared at each other, and the only sound was the dripping of rain off the trees. Then Jordan put a shaky hand to his face, turned and strode off toward the river.

Dillon burst into tears.

JORDAN SAT BY THE RIVER, his face buried in his hands. The bush rang with birdsong and he concentrated on identifying the calls…the bell-like warble of the tui, the throaty cry of the wood pigeon, kereru. His leg hurt—he'd forgotten about it until now. But he couldn't bring himself to care.

He heard Kate's light-footed approach and the rustle of grass as she sat beside him. He waited for her lecture, but she didn't say anything.

Jordan lifted his head and looked at her. There was wood ash in her hair, and she reeked of smoke, but her hazel eyes were as clear and calm as the river.

"Go ahead, I won't argue."

"I'm here to listen," she said.

"A bully," he said, a lump in his throat. "I'm the guy who protects people from bullies. What the hell got into me?"

"You imagined what could have happened and it scared you into overreacting."

He had. Oh, God, he *had* imagined losing Dillon. But also Kate. "That's a reason," he said brusquely, "not an excuse. I blamed Mike because I wanted to blame him, not because it was fair."

Wearily he rubbed his eyes. "I've been accusing him of jealousy, but I'm as bad. I just hid it better…until now."

Jordan shivered and realized he'd left his T-shirt at camp. He still had his

Swanndri tied around his waist, but he didn't want Kate to see his wound. He'd tend to that later.

"You know what the irony is? I convinced Claire to let Mike back into Dillon's life. I'd created the vacuum by not marrying her. It was my responsibility to help Dillon fill it, and he badly wanted to meet his real dad."

"It's natural Dillon got curious as he got older. That doesn't mean he lacked a father figure. You're obviously very close."

"We were."

"He'll forgive you, Jordan."

"But will Mike?" She didn't jump in with reassurances, and Jordan appreciated it.

"I met Dillon when he was two," he said. "I had a struggling new business, a grief-stricken mother and hormonal teenage sisters who hated their older brother for telling them they couldn't date. But Dillon was always happy to see me. I'd walk in the room and his face would light up...."

Jordan remembered Dillon's face a few minutes ago. Oh, God. Getting to his feet, he helped Kate to hers. For a moment he kept hold of her hand. "Thanks, Kate." He added gruffly, "Guess I need to start apologizing."

Jordan found Dillon throwing pebbles at an empty can, his small body taut with concentration. He looked like any other kid on the verge of growing up, hopelessly endearing to those who loved him. Then Dillon caught sight of him and became apprehensive.

That hurt. "You were right to defend your dad, Dil-boy. I *was* being a bully."

Dillon flung himself into Jordan's arms and they didn't speak for a few minutes. "I thought you'd be so mad at me."

"No, I'm mad at *me*. I'm sorry for scaring you. Are we friends again?"

Dillon pulled away and nodded, but he still looked anxious, and Jordan made a stab at the cause. "I'm going to apologize to your dad, too."

The boy finally relaxed.

"He may not be as forgiving as you are, though. I said some pretty mean things." Jordan thought it wiser to prepare Dillon, and Mike's reaction made him glad he did.

The man brushed off all Jordan's attempts to apologize. "Yeah, well, you made your feelings about me plain, so let's take it as a given that you think I'm a loser and I think you're an arrogant prick."

Jordan tried again. "Mike, I'm asking you to give me another chance." For a moment the other man hesitated, and Jordan started to hope. "Kate was right, we have been acting like two dogs with a bone—"

Mike glowered and Jordan realized the painful episode was the last thing he should have mentioned. "Oh, I get it. And now Dillon's chosen me, you've come with your tail between your legs, suddenly willing to share." He crossed his arms, widened his stance. "Maybe you're worried I'll tell Claire about your outburst and she'll reconsider your influence in his life. Well, mate, I can't *wait*. You be the loser for a change and see how it feels. Hopefully, it will teach you a little humility."

Jordan had sent Dillon down to the river for water; now he was very glad he had. Mike spun on his heel and went after the boy, and Jordan was left standing alone in the clearing.

There was a movement behind him and he turned to see Kate.

"Well, that went well," he said. She came over, took his face in her hands and kissed him hard.

"Don't give up yet," she said, and followed Mike. Dumbstruck, Jordan stared after her.

KATE COULDN'T BELIEVE she'd just kissed Jordan. Hurrying to the river, where there was safety in numbers, she castigated herself every step of the way.

What were you thinking, encouraging him like that?

I was only comforting him. "Yeah, right."

But he'd looked so lost, so vulnerable, so... It's temporary, she thought. He'll change back.

And if you help him he'll change back faster.

But how could she not? *Okay, help him then, but that's all.* She met the others coming back from the shore. "Mike, we need to talk."

"It's not a good time, Kate."

She realized Dillon was miserable again. Mike must have told him he hadn't accepted Jordan's apology, and she reined in her impatience. "Later then."

When they got back to camp, Jordan was sitting on a folding chair, the first-aid kit beside him. "Damn, I thought you'd all be down there longer," he said ruefully.

Kate gasped. Below his black boxers, dark, viscous blood oozed from a deep slash across his right thigh.

"I...fell."

Mike took control, taking the cloth

from him and wiping away the encrusted blood. Kate frowned as the wound started to look suspicious. "A fall, you say?"

"Lost my footing...rolled down a slope... scraped against a tree stump," Jordan said vaguely.

"You know," Kate said a little later, "this looks remarkably like one of the pictures in my pig book."

"Now you're being paranoid." Warily, Jordan watched Mike splash disinfectant onto a clean swab. "Don't you want to dilute that?"

Mike held it above his wound. "Last chance to change your story."

"I don't know what you—" Jordan hissed as Mike applied the swab.

Dillon was agog. "Does that hurt?"

"No," said Jordan through gritted teeth.

Cleaned up, the gash ran in a shallow jagged line almost the length of his thigh, carving deeper into the flesh near the top. The adults assessed it.

"Damn, I thought I'd get away without

stitches." Jordan reached into the first aid kit. "I have a thing about needles. Hopefully this one's small enough to pass under the phobia radar."

But he paled as he tried to thread the surgical needle with a shaky hand, and Mike confiscated it. "You're in luck. I've been a volunteer with the St. John's Ambulance Service for three years."

"Thank God. So you can also give me the tetanus jab?"

"Only if he tells the truth," Kate said to Mike.

They all waited.

"Okay, it was a pig," Jordan admitted. "But it was my fault."

"Cool," breathed Dillon.

Jordan told them the story, seemingly impervious to the fact that Mike was plying a needle in his leg. "And, Kate, I don't want it to affect the way you feel about…about…" His voice trailed off.

He was staring mesmerized at the needle. All the color left his face. His eyes rolled back and Kate caught him as he fell forward.

Dillon started to howl. "What's wrong with him?"

"It's okay, son, he just fainted," Mike said very calmly. "Kate, hold him steady for a minute while I finish the stitches."

Swallowing hard, she tightened her grip. Jordan's hair, soft against her cheek, smelled of wood smoke.

"Okay," said Mike finally. He cut the thread, then helped her place Jordan on his side in the recovery position. Almost immediately the patient groaned and tried to sit up.

Mike held him down. "You passed out. Lie still for a minute."

"Okay, guys," Jordan said weakly, "what'll it cost to keep this quiet?"

Dillon got all excited. "I want a Play-Station."

"It's yours."

"Don't talk crazy," Mike snapped. "Turn over and I'll give you the tetanus shot."

The color coming back to Jordan's face left it again. "I think I can only handle one needle a day."

"Don't be frightened," said Kate, enjoying being the fearless one for a change. Shooting her an evil look, Jordan rolled over. She stared at that fabulous swell of muscle under his boxers and her sense of superiority vanished.

With an effort she wrenched her eyes away and started clearing up the mess.

"Don't be surprised if I pass out again," Jordan warned.

"Take your mind off it," Mike said briskly. "Talk through it."

"Are you saying we've got something left to talk about, Mike?"

He didn't answer and Kate looked up. His face was stony as he prepared the needle.

"Tell me that river story again," Dillon suggested. "And whatever you do, don't *look.*" His dad was squeezing the air out of the syringe.

Obediently, Jordan cradled his face in his arms, and Kate caught her breath as the muscles bunched there. "Two great mountains," he began, "Tongariro and Taranaki, fought for the love of the beautiful Mount Pihanga."

Mike pushed up the boxers, exposing a taut creamy buttock, and she turned her back. "Taranaki lost," Jordan continued softly, "and, wild with grief, tore a path through this land as he headed toward the setting sun—*ouch!* At the ocean he turned north, ending up on the west coast, where he still nurses his broken heart. From the victor, Tongariro, a spring rose, which filled and healed the wound Taranaki had made in his flight—the mighty river Whanganui."

"Very romantic, I'm sure." Kate was still struggling to forget the image of his butt. "From what I've read, the land of the region was formed a million years ago, and the strata—"

"Spare me your prosaic facts." Jordan

rolled over and sat up. "You were all logic and science as a kid, weren't you? Cottoned on to the Easter bunny at three years old, probably, and at six made it your duty to denounce Santa to other little kids."

"At six, I measured the chimney and posted him a diet sheet so that he'd fit come Christmas," she said.

He smiled at her. She was still smoke smudged and dirty, with no clothes to change into. He had no right to look at her as if it didn't matter.

"You mean Santa's not real?" Dillon said plaintively, and everyone froze. His face broke into a grin. "You guys are so lame! I'm *twelve.*"

"And filthy," said Kate after they'd stopped laughing. "We all are. Question is, what am I going to wear while I wash these clothes?"

The somber mood reasserted itself. "A T-shirt of Dillon's." Jordan looked at Mike's small frame. "Some pants of Mike's and that Swanndri you love so

CHAPTER FIFTEEN

DILLON NEEDED TO TALK to Jordan, but he didn't want his dad around and the chance didn't come until right before dinner, when Mike went for more firewood.

Jordan was cooking some kind of stew over the stove, and Kate was reading aloud to him from her killer pig book. Dillon had been enjoying the teasing, but as soon as Dad disappeared, butterflies started in his stomach and he couldn't concentrate.

But Jordan always said if you had to do something it was better to jump right in, so Dillon took a deep breath and asked if they could have a talk by themselves. Kate said, "I'll stir the stew."

Jordan looked at him and stopped smiling. "Let's go into one of the tents."

But when they were sitting facing each other in the greenish gloom, Dillon didn't know how to start.

"It's okay," Jordan said. "You can say anything to me."

"You know how I stood up for Dad before."

"Yeah, you did the right thing."

"And he won't let you say sorry to him, and he still ha…doesn't like you."

Jordan nodded.

"Maybe for a little while, after this trip—" Dillon started playing with the zipper on the puffy green sleeping bag "—we shouldn't see each other." He looked anxiously at Jordan, whose face was completely expressionless. "It's not that I want to," Dillon said, blinking hard, "but…"

"You're tired of all the conflict. It's okay, Dil."

"No, it's not that. Something happened to Dad when he was young that I'm not allowed to tell you about." Dillon watched the zipper slide up and down until it caught on some fabric and stuck. He handed it to Jordan, who freed it and handed it back. "But it was bad and, well, he kinda needs me on his side...." His voice trailed off.

"And I don't," Jordan finished calmly. "It's the right decision, Dil-boy, and—" he cleared his throat "—I'm proud of you."

All Dillon's worries rolled off his shoulders. "So I haven't hurt your feelings?"

Jordan reached out and ruffled his hair. "C'mon, mate, Kate's probably burning the stew."

KATE HAD HEARD EVERY WORD and it was breaking her heart. Quickly she lifted the hem of Jordan's Swanndri and wiped away her tears.

It smelled faintly of him, and for a moment she buried her face in the coarse wool, then realized what she was doing and dropped it like a hot potato.

"We're starving," said Jordan behind her. *If he can be brave, so can I.* She swung around with a smile. He returned it, but there were lines around his blue eyes.

"So am I." Mike dumped a stack of wood by the fire. "That should see me through the night."

Kate resisted the urge to fling the ladle at him. "Then let's eat," she said, and dished up.

Mike and Dillon were the only ones with any appetite. Jordan noticed Kate pushing her food around the plate. "What's wrong?" His gaze flicked between her and the tent, and comprehension dawned on his face.

"Nothing," she lied. "Hey, Dillon, want to play Truth or Dare again tonight?"

"Sure."

"I'm not in the mood, guys," Jordan said. Mike agreed with him.

Kate ignored them both. "Last night you two didn't get to finish being nice to each other. You still owe me three minutes."

The two men stared at her, and even Dillon blinked. She ignored them all.

"Mike, last night we had you. Now it's Jordan's turn to answer questions."

Jordan pushed his plate aside and stood up. "This isn't funny, Kate."

"Sit," she said, in the same tone she'd used on her siblings when they were younger. Jordan sat. "Mike, you said when Dillon wanted to start seeing you again, Claire said no initially, and then changed her mind."

"Yeah, what's your point?"

She turned back to Jordan. "Who talked her into it?"

Jordan squirmed. "Does it matter?"

Dillon looked puzzled. "Wasn't it me?"

"Jordan," Kate asked again, "who talked Claire into letting Mike see Dillon?"

"I did, but—"

She cut him off. "Thank you, that's all." She couldn't let him qualify it…or say he regretted it. Kate looked back at Mike, who appeared stunned. "This is the man who gave you your second chance," she said. "I figure you owe *him* one, don't you?"

The fire hissed as it bit into green wood. Kate held her breath and waited.

Mike turned his head. "Are you going to make another effort to reconcile with your dad?"

Her heart sank. "That's blackmail."

"If you're going to talk the talk, then you need to walk the walk."

She looked at Dillon, then at Jordan, who were clearly both wondering what the hell was going on. "I'll try, but I'm making no promises."

"Then we understand each other," said Mike. He leaned forward and threw another chunk of wood on the fire. Sparks flew like fireflies. "You know, it's too bloody cold to sleep outside tonight. Okay if I share your tent, Jordan?"

"KATE?"

Over her shoulder she shot Jordan a wary look. Mike had already gone to bed, and she was following Dillon, who'd stayed up way too late playing cards.

Jordan knew she didn't want to be alone with him. "Come back a minute."

"I'm really tired…"

"I want to thank you."

She kissed Dillon, who was yawning widely. "I won't be far behind you, Dil-boy." Hearing his nickname for Dillon on her lips made Jordan grin. She came back to the fire, hesitated, then sat on the other side of it. Jordan found that very interesting.

"I owe you," he said.

She mumbled, embarrassed. He found it captivating that Kate Brogan could be shy.

"I didn't know you were estranged from your father."

Her face took on a haunted expression. "Guess you should have hired a better private investigator."

"You didn't want to say yes to letting him back into your life. You did it for us, me and Dillon."

She moistened her lips. "I only said I'd try."

"And you looked like someone facing

the electric chair. You listened to me today. Let me listen tonight."

She stared into the fire for so long he thought she'd forgotten him. "My father was a womanizer," she said in a low voice. "Even on the day my mother died he was with another woman. I used to cover Dad's tracks until I realized Mum knew about his affairs. She died without ever confronting him."

Angrily, she brushed some tears away. "His sick wife couldn't give him sex anymore, so he went elsewhere. Who am I kidding? I'll never forgive him."

"Did your father always cheat on your mother?"

Jordan could see his question baffled her. "No, he was always a flirt, but the affairs began when Mum got ill."

She shivered. Jordan poked the ash-covered embers with a stick. They pulsed like glowworms in the chill night air.

"When my father was dying," he said, "Mum suddenly started getting us to do things for Dad that she'd done for him all our lives. Like giving him a haircut and scrubbing his back in the bath. She and Dad used to listen to this radio program every night. She came up with excuses why it was better for one of us to sit with him."

He tossed the stick on top of the embers. "Dad said she was trying to mitigate the pain of losing him. It only lasted a couple of weeks, then she reinvested, and when he died they were closer than ever. She suffered terribly for the first couple of years afterward, but she says he was worth it."

"You think that maybe my dad was trying to prove he could live without Mum before he had to?"

"It's something to think about."

There was another silence. "You said I was like your father," Jordan said frowning.

"No," she hurried to assure him, "at least…not in that way. It's more your recklessness, your disregard of consequences, using your charisma to manipulate people. Your arrogance…"

She seemed to be winding into a list, rather than out of one, so Jordan interrupted with the question he desperately needed an answer to. "But you don't doubt my morals anymore?"

"No, or your heart. You'll make a good trustee."

It seemed ironic that she knew the state of his heart, considering he'd never been less sure of it. Jordan rarely thought about love, but now he wondered what its symptoms were—and if there was a cure. But lust? That was an emotion a guy could understand. "So," he said, "you kissed me this afternoon."

"Sunstroke."

"It was cloudy."

"I wanted to see if you'd turn into a prince."

He flashed her his wickedest grin. "And voilà."

Kate stood and brushed a few ashes off her pants.

Jordan stopped joking. "Give me a good reason," he said, "and don't make it Peter."

"Okay. Even believing that you didn't know your lover was married—"

"Thank you."

"—and…" she hesitated "…assuming Peter and I weren't engaged, let's measure your cost- benefit ratio."

He started to laugh. "I didn't bring a ruler."

She persevered. "I'm a woman who likes to get all the facts together before making an investment decision. How many women have you dated in the past twelve months?"

She was being so schoolmarmish, Jordan couldn't help himself. "Can I borrow your fingers and toes?"

"Promiscuity at your age is a sign of immaturity, not to mention dangerous for sexual health."

"Four, but I only slept with one of them." Chiefly because he'd been too busy with the business, but Kate didn't need to know that. "You're looking at a serial monogamist."

"Really." She sounded skeptical. "What's the longest you've been in a relationship since you broke up with Claire? What was that, eight years ago?"

"Six months." She raised a brow and he added reluctantly, "If you include three months when I was overseas. But we talked on the phone."

Kate folded her arms. "I rest my case."

Jordan wasn't deterred. "Fight all you want," he said, "but it's going to happen, Kate, and you know it."

CHAPTER SIXTEEN

IT WAS ONLY WHEN the canoe scraped across the long bank of fine river pebbles with a sound like fingernails on a blackboard that Kate realized she'd been paddling on autopilot.

She turned to look at Jordan. "Why have we stopped?" They'd only been in the water a couple of hours.

"Got a lot on your mind today, Kate?" He grinned at her, a complicit smile full of promise.

"No," she said shortly. "I didn't get much sleep last night and I'm tired." She shouldn't have said that, either. They both knew the cause of her restlessness.

Mike and Dillon beached beside them. "What's up?" True to his word, Mike had dropped all his antagonism. The only under-currents this morning had been in the river.

"I need to assess a hazard."

Following the direction of Jordan's gaze, Kate saw a place where the sprawling beach had created a bottleneck of white water. "It doesn't look too hard," she ventured. "Not compared to some we've navigated." She experienced a brief stab of pride; she'd come a long way in a few days.

"It wouldn't be without the snag," Jordan agreed, "but see the tree that's fallen just in front of it?"

She looked again and saw a spindly branch in the water creating a V in the current. "That little thing?"

Jordan didn't answer; he was studying the riverbanks. "Mike, I want Kate and Dillon to walk. You and I will take the canoes down." He started unpacking one of the wet suits. Mike blinked, then beamed at Kate with too much smugness for her liking.

"Wait a minute, why can't I take one

down with you?" she said. "I'm as competent as Mike, aren't I?"

Jordan's hesitation was so brief she nearly missed it. "No."

"Liar." She pulled out her own wet suit.

Jordan folded his arms. "You're not doing it, Kate."

"Tell me honestly," she challenged, "what are the risks?"

"From what I can see? Small," he admitted. "But that's the problem—most of the new snag is submerged. By the way the water's flowing around it, I think it will be okay, but there's a chance we'll get pushed left."

Kate looked to where the water surged against the canyon wall, creating a backwash of large waves.

"If that happens," said Jordan, "we'll capsize. However slight, there's always the risk of injury."

"There aren't any exposed rocks to smash into," she said, "and if we fall in I'll float on my back, feet first, so I don't catch them on anything that will drag me under."

"Let me guess—*When Rapids Attack.*" He was trying not to smile.

She pressed her advantage. "I'm a good swimmer, Jordan, probably better than Mike. Tell me honestly, is there a reason, other than my being female, for not letting me go down?"

"You're being female has nothing to do with it."

"Then why?"

"I don't know," he conceded. For some reason the idea of Kate taking a minor risk made him feel sick.

"Then I'm going down." She disappeared into the trees to get dressed.

Dillon said, "If she can go then why—"

"Don't even start, Dillon," said Jordan, pointing him toward the bank. "And what are you smiling at?" he snapped at Mike.

"Nothing."

Kate came back in her wet suit, looking like a cross between a mermaid and a seal.

She hauled on her life jacket again. Jordan checked it twice and spent the next five minutes outlining his approach strategy and reiterating safety instructions. "If we tip, swim straight to shore. Don't worry about the canoe, I'll take care of it. Mike, you and I will go first."

Kate watched them slip through the gap without incident, and wondered why Jordan was making such a fuss. It seemed easy enough. She told him that when he walked back. "You just concentrate," he warned her.

"Piece of cake."

THEY FELL OUT. It was her fault.

Blinded by spray, Kate had wiped her eyes and the current ripped the paddle out of her other hand. The canoe shot into the backwash and a wave crashed over the bow, filling it with icy water. Maneuverability lost, the craft spun astern and the next wave flipped it.

Kate had no time to take a deep

breath. One second she was grabbing for her paddle, the next tumbling in a pounding swirl of white water, with no idea which way was up. *So much for floating on my back.*

She popped to the surface and gasped a lungful of air, frantically scanning for Jordan. Her terror gave way to relief when she spotted him beside the canoe. He waved and wrestled the craft toward shore. Kate swam to help him, and over the noisy churning he yelled, "Swim to safety, *now.*"

Obediently, she staggered into the shallows. Jordan floated past, fully occupied with the canoe. Beyond him, their paddles drifted lazily downstream.

Instinctively, Kate dived back into the water. They were easy to overtake, but the current, swifter than it looked, swept her around a bend in the river.

The gorge rose steeply here, with few egress points. She kicked furiously toward one, and ended up nudging a steeper bank downstream. Tossing the paddles onto shore, she grabbed a tree root and hauled herself up the incline, grimacing as her bare shins scraped on stones embedded in the clay.

Wet and bedraggled, she rested until she got her breath, then scrambled to her feet. This narrow section of gorge lay in deep shade, which colored the river inky black and gave the air a graveyard chill.

Elated that she'd saved the paddles, Kate didn't care. So what if she had to walk back through a half kilometer of inhospitable bush? As long as she stuck to the river she wouldn't get lost. Doubtfully, she regarded the immediate area and saw that the other shore offered a better route.

Shivers racked her body as she gauged the distance to the opposite bank. Best to go now, before hypothermia set in. Bundling up the paddles, Kate slid awkwardly down the slope.

"Stay *there,* damn it!" Glancing upstream, Kate saw Jordan paddling toward her, Mike and Dillon behind him. Even across the stretch of water she could see he was furious. "What the hell were you thinking?"

Kate held up the paddles proudly. "I got them," she called, then noticed he held one. Before she could process that, the canoe nudged the bank. "Get in." He steadied the craft with expert strokes while she scrambled aboard, then struck out for a clearing on the opposite shore. "I *specifically* told you to swim to safety."

Huddled on the seat, Kate couldn't stop shivering. Somewhere along the way she'd ripped the leg of her wet suit. Great, now nothing she owned was in one piece. "I s-saw the paddles disappearing…I never thought we'd carry spare ones."

"That's the trouble with you—you don't think." The canoe hit the shore with a bump. Jordan jumped out and hauled it across the pebbles, with her still in it.

"It's just as well my b-bottom's

numb," she protested, "because this would really h-hurt."

He lifted her out of the boat. "Guess there's no point in spanking you, then. I'd want it to hurt." He set her on her feet, then tightened his arms around her. "Don't *ever* frighten me like that again."

She clung to his warmth. "I'm a strong swimmer. There wasn't any risk." He was shaking, too; she could feel it. "Jordan?"

He bent his head. "Stop fighting this, Kate."

His mouth was warm against her ear; his breath tickled the fine hairs at her nape. A shiver that had nothing to do with the cold ran down Kate's spine. She only needed to turn her head to kiss that mouth, to ignite the passion that was always a heartbeat away, no matter how she tried to deny it.

Her head turned of its own volition.

There was a shout to her left and the other canoe beached. Kate stepped back as Dillon jumped out and ran toward them. She'd never been so pleased to see anyone in her life.

She hadn't slept much last night, but she had reached a decision. Regardless of their new understanding, regardless of her immense attraction to him, Jordan was still a loose cannon, with no history of fidelity or stability or any of the things she needed. And she wasn't getting involved with him.

JORDAN DOZED in the sun, his T-shirt a makeshift pillow. His mouth looked fuller without the sardonic smile that always hovered there when he was awake. And his long, curved lashes cast shadows on his cheeks, smooth above the burnished stubble on his jaw.

God, he was sexy. Kate wrenched her eyes away and took another bite of her apple. *Calm down, Eve,* she told herself. *Remember there was a fall at the end of the Garden of Eden story.*

"Oh, no," Mike cried, "Jordan's fainted

again!" He and Dillon cracked up laughing; Kate chuckled.

The man in question stretched lazily, rolled onto his side and propped himself up on an elbow, his hair falling over his broad brown shoulders. "Aren't you getting sick of that joke yet?"

The three of them looked at one another and laughed again. "Nope," said Mike.

Absentmindedly, Kate scratched a mosquito bite on her leg and cringed at the stubble. Jordan must be desperate if he found her attractive, looking like this. She might be scrubbed civilized with the daily assistance of a billy of hot water and a flannel, but she had to look a mess in Dillon's tight T-shirt, and the old track pants of Mike's, and with her hair a riot of curls.

It had rained off and on all night and morning, and this break in the clouds wasn't enough to dry out her own clothes. On the other hand, paddling through the wilderness with lipstick on was plainly ridiculous—unless she wanted to impress someone—which she didn't. Oh, God.

Kate flung herself down on her blanket. She only had to keep her traitorous emotions in check for the next twenty-four hours. Once she was back in the city she'd come to her senses. She tried to conjure a picture of her real life, but the image wavered. *No service,* she thought sadly, closing her eyes. The navy cotton T-shirt acted as a heat sink, catching the sun's rays and radiating them through her exhausted body.

Dimly she heard Jordan say, "Okay, Mike, I can see I'm going to have to buy your silence. What's your price?"

A raindrop woke her, a cold splash on her face, and Kate opened her eyes to see gunmetal-gray clouds charging across the sky like tanks.

"She's awake," she heard Dillon say excitedly. "Kate, come and say goodbye."

Obediently, she got to her feet. Wait a minute…goodbye?

His life jacket on, Dillon sat in the canoe, paddle at the ready. Jordan was explaining a map to Mike, who was also wearing his life jacket. "When you come to this S-shaped bend, you'll see a rock formation to your right."

"Where are you going?" Kate managed to keep the panic out of her voice as she hurried forward.

"There's an ancient Maori *pa* site up this tributary that Mike wants to see." Jordan pointed to the stream flowing into the river. "He and Dillon are going to check it out."

Another raindrop splashed on Kate's shoulder. "Well, let's get going then."

Mike looked guilty. "Well, we're kinda using it as a chance for a little father-son bonding, Kate, if that's okay."

"Sure." She glanced at Jordan to see how he was taking it. He looked very relaxed. "In fact, I think that's great."

"That was Mike's price for keeping the needlephobia quiet." Jordan read her mind. "It seemed fair."

"Wow," she said, "I'm impressed. You two are really acting like grown-ups. Well, have a good time and we'll see you later."

A look flashed between the two men that reminded her more of two impish boys. Grinning, Mike got in the canoe. "See you tomorrow at the rendezvous, then. Shove us off, will you, Kate?"

Instead, she clutched the gunwale. "Tomorrow?"

"Yeah, we're camping overnight," Dillon enthused. "It's gonna be so cool."

"You seem to be having a bit of trouble there, Red." Jordan unwrapped her fingers from the gunwale and gave the canoe a light push. It floated into the river, and Mike and Dillon began paddling. The occasional raindrops became a light drizzle.

Kate realized Dillon was waving, so she waved back.

"Well," said Jordan, "that just leaves you and me to act like grown-ups."

She remembered the look that had passed

between him and Mike, and her temper began to rise. "This is a setup, isn't it?"

"I thought you wanted us to work together?"

Her waving to Dillon became frenzied. "You low-down, sneaking—"

"Relax, Kate," he soothed. "Mike wants to spend time alone with Dillon and I want to spend time alone with you. Other than that, the ball's in your court."

Strangely, that thought didn't hold the reassurance it once had. Dillon and Mike disappeared from sight.

"It's raining," she said. "We need to make camp."

"We'll push on…our last campsite is still two hours ahead."

Alarm bells started ringing in Kate's head. "Wait a minute." She stared at Jordan in horror. "We only have two tents, and if they've taken one…"

CHAPTER SEVENTEEN

IT RAINED AND it rained and it rained. It felt as if it had always been raining.

Mechanically, Kate punched the paddle forward into the water, too tired to wipe the drip off the end of her nose. She distracted herself by thinking of other words for being wet. *Drenched, soaked, saturated, sodden.*

The rain had even dampened her resentment toward Jordan. But it hadn't been extinguished. It flared again now. "There's one solution to this," she yelled over her shoulder. "You're sleeping outside tonight."

"In this weather? You're crazy." He grinned. "What's the matter, Red, scared you won't be able to keep your hands off me?"

Kate gritted her teeth and resumed

paddling, replacing water words with killing words. *Shoot, blow up, spear, impale.*

The wetter they got, the more odiously sanguine Jordan became, whistling as the clouds darkened and the rain escalated to a pounding deluge.

When Jordan finally called it a day, dusk was falling, cloaking the icy rain.

Muddy puddles forced Kate to detour onto slippery gradients as she trudged up and down the slope leading to their campsite, unloading the canoe while Jordan remained at the top, pitching the tent.

Water trickled down the back of her neck and exhaustion made her careless as she jogged down the hill on her fourth run. So what if she fell? Lying anywhere would be a relief.

Famished, she stopped to open the food barrel, but her hands slipped as she wrestled for a grip on the lid. Cursing, she balanced it on the gunwale and finally succeeded in getting it off.

Her eyes fell on the brandy and she pounced, her chilled fingers fumbling with the steel cap. She took a swig and grimaced, but then the fire hit her belly. *Ah, heat.* Rain pounded on her upturned face as she took two more gulps. Feeling more cheerful, Kate seized the barrel and returned uphill.

Jordan passed her going the other way, and she sucked in her breath to hide the brandy fumes, then castigated herself for cowardice. As if his invasion into her life wasn't enough, he now exercised an insidious influence over her behavior, as well. The barrel landed among the bags with a thud.

Forgetting that her work was done, she half skidded, half stumbled down the slope and discovered the canoe empty and Jordan tipping the water out of it. *Now I have to climb this bloody hill again—and for nothing.*

Skirting a large puddle, she slipped into the muddy wallow. *What the hell, I can't get any wetter.* Her boots squelched as she walked straight through it. She was halfway up the hill when Jordan called, "Hey, Red, aren't you forgetting something?"

Kate looked down to where he stood at the water's edge. "The canoe," he explained patiently. "I need your help to move it to higher ground."

She waved a dismissive hand. "Let it be swept away. I never want to see it again."

"I know just the place we can build a cabin."

Muttering, Kate stomped back down. Jordan had stripped to his boxers, and the rain slicked the chiseled muscles of his chest and abdomen.

He noticed her staring. "No point wearing wet clothes. You might want to do the same."

She tore her eyes away from his biceps. "Some of us prefer modesty."

"So a wet T-shirt competition doesn't have any appeal?" Kate glanced down, saw her nipples darkly outlined under the wet cotton, and slammed her palms over her breasts. "Pity." Jordan shrugged. "You would have won hands down."

"You are…" Kate searched for words scorching enough to melt that grin right off his face, but she was too tired to be clever. While she was thinking, the rain drizzled to a stop. At Jordan's signal, she hoisted her end of the canoe. He moved to the middle to minimize her load, using her as a balance rather than a bearer. For some reason that made her madder.

"Let's go." He moved lightly over the rough ground, and Kate quickened her stride to keep up with him. Partway up, he indicated an area to one side of the track.

The canoe landed in the grass with a sound like a soft sigh, and Kate knew how it felt. She stretched to loosen her back, then hurriedly crossed her arms as Jordan's gaze followed the movement. "Not one word," she warned.

His eyes widened innocently and she saw exactly how he must've defended himself as a boy. Except he was one hundred percent adult male. "Okay, mister, you go first." From the way his wet boxers outlined his ass, she wasn't letting him walk behind her, either.

Resolutely, Kate looked north and was captivated by the undulating muscles of his upper body. One foot slid out from under her, she lurched forward and landed with a squelch in the soft clay.

For a moment she lay with her cheek glued to the mud, the smell of rotting forest sharp in her nostrils. Then she hauled herself upright.

Jordan avoided her baleful stare as he scanned her for injury. "Are you hurt?"

Was that a tremor of laughter? Kate stiffened. "Only my pride…and my temper."

He turned away too quickly and she narrowed her eyes. The shaking in those shoulders was unmistakable. All the week's frustration exploded in a cleansing rage.

Dropping to a squat, Kate grappled for wet clay, which she molded into a ball with icy fingers. She stood and hurled it with all her strength, and it landed with a splat between his broad shoulders. Jordan stopped dead. She watched, entranced, as the clod slid in a deeply satisfying manner down his back.

Slowly he turned to face her. "Kate," he warned softly. *Smack*. The second clod hit him full in the chest. She laughed aloud.

"Kate." His tone was pained.

Whack. The third landed just below his navel. He winced and she knew with a thrilling terror she'd gone too far. "You realize," he said, "this means war?"

His first missive slammed into her back as she high-tailed it in retreat. "Back to being a coward, huh?" The challenge arrested her midflight. She knew he was being deliberately provocative, knew it even as she bent rashly to the task of forming mud balls to wipe that smirk off his face.

But she was outclassed. Every one of his missiles hit its target—her—while only one in three of hers found its mark. In the end, Kate opted for a kamikaze attack, molding as many balls as she could and rushing at him, firing on the run. Jordan stood his ground and she charged into him, panting and laughing, and smeared the remains of her arsenal on his chest.

His stillness awoke Kate to the fact that her rough plastering had become caresses, and her hands faltered to a halt on his strong pectorals.

Blushing, she jerked away, but Jordan's hands caught hers in a viselike grip and returned them to his torso. "Don't stop, I like it." The huskiness in his voice quivered through her like a pulse, and Kate lifted her gaze. Big, big mistake. It was like connecting into the national power grid.

With an unsteady laugh, she shifted focus to the muddy streaks across Jordan's face. "You look like a kid playing cowboys and Indians."

Mud creased into smile lines as he grinned. "So do you." With unhurried deliberation he ran a thumb along her jawline, and Kate closed her eyes, weak with lust. *Step away from the guy. Remember what you decided.*

Under her splayed hands, the pliant warmth of his naked chest sent waves of feeling surging through her.

Swallowing hard, Kate opened her eyes. Jordan's head was inches from her own and she raised her face to his, compelled by his heartbeat under her hand, as frantic as hers. Their lips met—and her hesitancy was over.

Whatever she'd weathered today paled in comparison to the storm that shook her now. Jordan's mouth was a lifeline, and she clung to his body, giving in to her need, which only grew as she surrendered to it.

His lips were chilled, but his tongue was hot. Their teeth hit clumsily as Kate wound her arms around his neck and hauled him closer. It didn't matter. She felt alive, wild…pagan.

The rain started again, slowly at first, then fast and hard, pelting their entwined bodies, its iciness caresses heightening the erotic heat. Jordan trailed kisses down her throat, and cool drops of water landed on Kate's tongue as her mouth fell open in a gasp of pleasure.

His hands rose to her breasts. "I've wanted to do this all day," he rasped and bent his head, teasing her nipples through the wet T-shirt.

When it was too much, she grabbed his hair and hauled him up. Laughing softly, she saw how the dirt from her shirt decorated his face with daubs and streaks of red-brown. The laugh caught in her throat, as their eyes met. How could a man be so sexy covered in mud?

Recklessly, she pressed her mouth to his. Their kisses grew deeper and increasingly erotic, foreshadowing the thrust and surrender of sex.

I should stop this, she thought dimly, while her muddy fingers traced the muscles of his back, delighting in the texture of his skin, slippery with rain.

As her hands came to rest on the curve of his buttocks, Kate struggled for sanity. *I must stop this,* she thought again, and slid her fingers under the waistband of his wet boxers.

"Stop." Voice cracking, Jordan took her hands and placed them firmly behind her back, then moved away two paces, breathing deeply. *What the hell am I doing?* Every soft, throaty sound she made as he kissed her was driving him to take her right here in the middle of the clearing—rain, mud and all.

And she'd hate him for it afterward.

It didn't matter how willing and eager she might be now. Passion wasn't enough for Kate, and this recklessness had been alcohol induced—he'd tasted the brandy. She liked to base her decisions on cold, hard reason.

As opposed to hot, hard male, he thought bitterly. She made him think about things he'd always reacted to on instinct. He hated it. He might not care for consequences, but Kate did, and that was what mattered now. He made himself say it. "What about Peter?"

"Peter?" she repeated. Mud streaked her flushed face, her hair was a mass of dark tendrils, her lips were swollen from his kisses and her eyes were dreamy with lust.

"Your fiancé, remember?" His voice cracked again, this time like a whip. Kate stared at him. "Go get cleaned up before we do something you'll regret."

"Oh, stop being so bloody noble. It doesn't suit you."

His lips quirked. "Is that the alcohol speaking or has it brought out the real you? I can taste the brandy, Kate."

"I'm not *drunk*…only tipsy. And Peter and I are finished. He broke off our engagement before I came on this trip."

His eyes intent on her face, Jordan said, "I'm sorry."

She started to laugh. "No, you're not.

You've been telling me to dump him this whole trip."

"I wanted it to be your choice, Kate, not his."

Damned if she'd accept Jordan's pity at this point. Kate shrugged. "I'm adopting your philosophy—seize the day. Or in this case, the man." Minutes ago she would have made love in the mud; now all this talking had left her uncertain and a little sick. Still, she put her arms around his waist and said brightly, "I figure you owe me some fun, don't you?"

Jordan held her gaze so long her cheeks started to ache from holding the smile. Gently he cupped her face in his hands. "Babe, I'm not going to seduce you until you're sure it's what you want."

And Kate suddenly thought, *I can trust this man.* It made her feel light hearted. "I do want you," she said.

Jordan shook his head. "I don't think you know what you want right now." Turning her around, he gave her a little push. "I'm going to stand here and wash off the mud. Go behind the tent and do the same. Then find some dry clothes in my bag."

Kate found herself walking away. Behind the tent she stood in the downpour, then dragged off her T-shirt and went through the motions of wiping herself off. *I'm in love with him.* No, that was impossible. Good grief, she'd only *liked* him two days. She'd been engaged to another guy last week—*whom I didn't love*. But Jordan absolutely wasn't her type. He also wasn't into commitment. *Okay. I'm in lust.*

An idea came to Kate that frightened the life out of her. "I can't do *that*."

For a long minute she wavered, then with shaking hands removed the rest of her wet clothes. Her whole life she'd avoided taking risks, and she was sick of it. For once she was going to close her eyes and jump into the unknown. Get messy, get real, be real…be vulnerable. Okay, he wasn't marriage material, but as Lucy had said, he was a great guy to have fun with. And wasn't Kate overdue for some fun?

Naked, she stood in the rain. "You can do this, Kate," she affirmed through chattering teeth. Taking a deep breath, she walked back, terror dragging at her ankles with every step. *Of course he'll reject you. You're a madwoman.*

Of course he'll reject me, I'm a madwoman.

Then she saw Jordan, and all her doubts evaporated. Eyes closed, he stood with his face upturned to the sky, water clinging to his long lashes, plastering his hair to his back and dripping off his hard body.

A wild confidence surged through Kate's veins, unexpected and freeing. Hearing her approach, he opened his eyes. She saw a flash of astonishment, quickly replaced by a wary stillness.

She stopped when her naked body was inches away from his, and trailed purposeful fingers down the planes of his face. Jordan's stillness grew more marked.

Kate didn't look away, compelling his acquiescence as her fingers skimmed over the rough stubble on his jaw, the pulse hammering in his throat and the corded muscle where his neck met his shoulders.

Down the broad chest she slid her hand, pausing to tease a nipple. Jordan sucked in a breath, but stood like a rock. She could see him resist the urge to give in to her.

She dropped her hand farther, under the waistband of his boxers, and his eyes widened. "Let's be crystal clear about this." She tightened her hold and swayed toward him until her nipples lightly grazed his chest. "*I* am doing the ravishing. Explicit enough for you?"

CHAPTER EIGHTEEN

ALL THE BREATH WAS squeezed from Kate's body as Jordan jerked her hard against him. He quivered under her hand and she gasped.

"What do you think?" he growled, bending to lick a raindrop from her wet cheek.

"I think if you don't take me now, I'll die." She watched the male arrogance return to his face, and thrilled with an answering female power. Lightning streaked the sky, followed by a clap of thunder. *Oh boy,* she thought, *this isn't Saturday night in bed with the lights out.*

Without another word, Jordan picked her up and carried her to the tent. The rain was buffeting the thin nylon, and he put her down to zip up the opening. Kate was suddenly conscious of her naked body dripping water onto the floor, and she rummaged for towels, more to cover herself than dry off.

When she turned back he was half crouched at the entrance, watching her. "Change your mind?"

"No." Still, she couldn't stop shaking.

Jordan seized the towels, threw one on the air bed and sat her on it, then knelt in front of her and started vigorously drying her off. "You're freezing."

"This wet dog thing you do…" she complained through chattering teeth. More than cold was making her tremble.

"Do me," he invited, and her tension eased as she gave back as good as she got, and soon they were both rubbed rosy and chuckling.

Jordan flipped the towel over their heads and kissed her under it, and somehow ended up kneeling between her thighs with her body pulled intimately against his.

It was the most incredibly erotic sensation Kate had ever experienced—his tongue teasing hers, the warmth of his hands on her lower back and the shocking heat of him pressed against her from groin to breast. The air under the towel grew steamy.

"Not fair," she murmured as he drew her closer, making her even more aware of her wanton position. "You're still dress— *oh*—" He'd thrust forward just enough that the silken slide of his boxers rubbed against… "Oh," Kate gasped again, and shoved the towel away, needing air.

"You like that?" He did it once more, and she tightened her legs around him to make him stop, because she was going to come apart and that rarely happened and couldn't possibly now. He wasn't even naked, and she wasn't going to feel this much, she'd already decided.

Tenderly, Jordan loosened her grip. In the near dark, he was a shadow only. A flash of lightning briefly illuminated his face. "For you," he said, and moved again, and she shattered—spectacularly, noisily, losing her grip on his shoulders and sprawling back onto the bed in a loose-limbed heap.

Gradually, Kate became aware of the wind shaking the rain off the tent, the thunder rumbling in the distance, the damp smell of the sleeping bag under her—and Jordan stroking her prickly legs, still bent ignominiously over the air bed.

She'd never had sex without being showered and smooth and made-up. Peter liked it that way; Kate thought she did, too. This raw vulnerability was outside her experience. For a moment she lay contented, thinking, *I've lost all my inhibitions.* Then Jordan turned on the lantern, flooding the tent with light. Yelping, she rolled over and scrambled for the opening of the sleeping bag.

"Oh no, you don't." He caught one flailing foot. "I've waited too long to look at you."

"I'm a mess."

"You're beautiful," he said, and the sincerity in his voice cut through her embarrassment. She sneaked a peek over her bare shoulder.

"At least take away your advantage." She nodded toward the boxers. Except he revealed another advantage when he casually shucked them off and dropped them on the tent floor.

"Better?"

The man was even more beautiful naked. His wound was bleeding slightly, and Kate took the opportunity to marshal her emotions. "That looks nasty. Let me dress it."

"Not quite the reaction a guy wants when he takes his pants off." Then he saw what she was looking at. "Damn. Well, I guess we can include nursing in foreplay."

She wasn't sure what he meant until he sat down in front of her and she realized she'd have to play medic inches away from his spectacular erection.

Kate blushed and started working clumsily on the injury. Jordan winced.

"I'm sorry, I'm not very…" What? Good at this? Adventurous? She had no idea what this man expected. Peter had been very particular about where he liked to be touched and how.

Jordan reached out and smoothed away her frown, making her jump, and she banged the wound again. "What did I say to make you so anxious?" he murmured.

Keeping her attention on his thigh, Kate positioned a cotton pad in place and taped it down. "Pete and I…well, we tried everything…at least once. But probably only to cross it off our list." Jordan laughed and she stiffened, hot with humiliation.

Immediately, he sobered. "Aah, Kate."

She steeled herself to look at him. His expression was very kind, which made things worse, but she forced herself to say it. "We were both shy… physically."

"I hadn't noticed, myself," he murmured.

Recalling her behavior minutes earlier, she felt even more exposed. Her ministrations were finished; unconsciously she wrapped her arms around herself.

Jordan stroked her hair, kissed her eyebrows, her eyelids, the tip of her nose. "I'm a bastard," he said, "because I'm happy there's still something I can give you—the knowledge that you're an incredibly sensual woman."

He dug his Swanndri out of his bag and pulled it over her head. "Let's start by making you comfortable."

Sitting her down, Jordan remade the bed, unzipping their two sleeping bags and laying them flat, then building makeshift pillows out of his clothes. He moved around the tent, still naked and completely relaxed, his hair falling over his broad shoulders.

Kate had never seen anyone so at ease with his body. The lantern cast a glow on his skin, a rich brown paling into cream below the tan line. Tiny golden hairs glinted on his strong legs and forearms and around his small puckered nipples, darkening where it arrowed down his flat stomach.

She watched the ripple and pull of sinew and muscle as he moved, and her reticence faded under the urge to touch him. Their eyes met and Jordan's pupils dilated as he read the direction of her thoughts. "You set the pace," he invited.

And because she was covered now, and more confident, Kate left the lantern on and touched him. Touched his fingers and wrists, slid her palms up his forearms to his biceps. Slowly her hands ranged over his body while she explored the different textures of his skin...rough and scarred here, soft there.

Jordan groaned appreciatively.

Encouraged, she caressed his powerful legs, reaching between them to cup and feel the weight of him, then ran her fingers up the ridges of his stomach to stroke the downy hair under his arms, so at odds with the rough stubble on his jaw and the wiry gold on his legs.

On the bed, she entwined her hands in his and lifted them over his head, just to see his biceps change shape, then kissed his eyebrows and his eyelids. "Girls' lashes," she teased, emboldened by his reaction to her caresses.

"At least mine aren't singed," he teased back, and she rubbed her cheek against the bristles on his jaw, then plundered his mouth. Laughter during lust was headier than any whispered words of intimacy for Kate. That sex could be so much fun was a revelation.

And when she'd finished touching him, she tasted. The freshness of rain, and mint and mud and man. She grew hot and sweaty under the Swanndri and hauled it off, relinquishing the eroticism of being clothed against his nakedness for the new one of skin to skin.

And then he was touching her, his long hair tickling as he worked his way down her body, exploring, trailing heat…teasing her breasts to tight peaks, moving lower.

She raised her head to protest as he parted her legs, saw his hair falling over her belly and the bunched muscles of his shoulders, and couldn't move, couldn't breathe, couldn't care about propriety.

The world closed in until there were only murmurs and the sound of their labored breathing, hot inside the chilly tent. Lost in this miraculous, fearless world, Kate murmured, "I love you."

KATE SLEPT, but Jordan couldn't, restlessly alive to her heat, her scent, the rhythm of her breathing as she nestled close to him. She'd said she loved him.

How had this happened? Why hadn't he had more warning, more chance to… What? Raise some barricades? The same ones she'd been knocking over the whole trip with her feistiness and kindness and sexiness and stubbornness and smart, funny mouth.

Gently he disentangled himself. He couldn't think while she was soft and yielding in his arms.

He should have realized that his

feelings had progressed beyond lust after those terrifying, heart-stopping minutes yesterday before he'd found her, standing wet and bedraggled on the riverbank, triumphantly holding the paddles above her head like a damn trophy.

The last time he'd thought he was in love with a woman he'd been wrong, and he'd hurt Claire very badly as a consequence. He didn't want to hurt Kate, though he doubted she'd let him. He'd always known she was a strong woman, but he hadn't appreciated how strong until he'd heard exactly what she'd had to overcome. It also explained why she'd resisted him for so long. She wanted emotional security, and Jordan wasn't a safe bet.

She was right. For eight years he'd avoided real intimacy.

He wound a strand of her hair around his finger and made a corkscrew curl. His throat tightened.

Damn it, Kate shouldn't have said she loved him. Jordan embraced his resentment. He wasn't ready to be shoved out of his comfort zone. He didn't even have a pair of training wheels.

Unable to resist it, he gently pulled Kate back into his arms and buried his face in her hair. *What if I can't be the guy you need?* he thought desperately. *Hell, I'm not ready.*

His business required constant travel, and the camp would soon need a lot of his energy. But letting her go… His arms tightened around her. Jordan stared into the dark for a long time before he found a solution. What they needed to do was to slow this down. Maybe that way he stood a better chance of quantifying his feelings for her, of controlling them. Of not blowing it.

KATE WOKE SLOWLY, letting sensations trickle into her consciousness, where she examined them idly before putting them aside like puzzle pieces to fit together later.

There was a radiant heater the length of her back. Her breasts were cold, though covered with something fine and soft.

She ached as though she'd been horse-back riding, which was silly because she was scared of horses and had never ridden anything bigger than—

An image slammed into her brain—Jordan in surrender to her, hands behind his head, powerful biceps exciting her to tease just a little more while he looked up at her astride him, his eyes narrowed in appreciative torment.

She opened her own a crack. His long hair lay across her breasts. She closed her eyes again quickly and wondered which feeling was strongest. Embarrassment, exhilaration, guilt, panic.

He was the only man she'd slept with other than Peter, and she didn't know what the etiquette was. It wasn't as if she could sneak home; they were in the middle of the forest, for Pete's—no, not Pete—for pity's sake. Jordan probably didn't even want her there—

Suddenly she lay flat on her back, his eyes inches from her own, his hair falling like a curtain, enclosing them in their own private world.

"You promised me, no regrets or self-recrimination."

"How did you know I was awake?"

"If you'd stiffened up any more, I could have used you as an ironing board." He looked at her swollen mouth with satisfaction. "I think that's probably the only thing we didn't do last night."

"Oh, God," croaked Kate, as she remembered she'd said that she loved him, and her passionate declaration had been met with silence.

Jordan rolled over onto his back, with her nerveless body gathered in his arms. "I think I've created a monster."

"Don't," she groaned, "I can't bear it."

"You're going to have to bear it." He slid his hand purposefully down her back. "I'm nowhere near done with you yet."

They had no future; still, her heart needed to confirm what her head already knew. Tracing a bull's-eye over his chest,

Kate said lightly, "So where do we go from here?"

She could feel the tension in his body, but he answered equally lightly, "Do we need a destination yet?"

She wrapped her pride closely around her. "Absolutely not. I'm barely out of a long-term relationship, and you…well, you're you."

If anything, he tensed up more. "What's that supposed to mean?"

"It's okay, Jordan, I have no expectations."

He paused before saying, "Last night you said you loved me."

"Oh, God, don't bring that up!" She forced a laugh. "Heat of the moment stuff."

He pulled her up so they were eye to eye. "You said it twice," he said slowly. "The second time when you were falling asleep."

Was he intent on humiliating her? Bent on self-protection now, she said, "Habit, sorry."

"Because of Peter." His tone was flat.

She'd never said it to Peter, but Kate seized the excuse. "I'm sure I'll stop soon."

Jordan's expression darkened. "Do you even want to see me again?"

"I don't know why you're making such a big deal about this," she said reasonably.

Neither did he. She was telling him he was a rebound guy, removing all pressure, and Jordan was furious. "Is this a one-night stand to you, Kate?"

She flinched. "No, but I'm not going to pretend we have a future. Let's keep this fun, keep it light, see what happens."

"And what if I don't want a relationship with you on those terms?"

"They're your terms," she said quietly, "and it's not just about what you want, is it, Jordan?"

She was very close to telling him to go to hell. Jordan made himself calm down. Why was he even arguing? She was right, those *were* his terms. And he should be counting himself lucky he had a woman who understood them.

"Okay," he said, "we'll see what happens…when I do this." He nipped her neck where he'd discovered she liked it, felt the shock of pleasure shudder through her.

"And this…" He trailed kisses down her body, stopping short of a nipple, watched it peak in anticipation under his slow, deliberate breaths. Kate stirred restlessly.

"Okay," she whispered, "you've made your point."

"I haven't even started." If all she wanted from him was a good time, then he was going to give her a very good time. So good she'd keep coming back for more.

IT WAS LATE MORNING before they were within sight of the small settlement that was their final destination. Only the fact that they were meeting Mike and Dillon had dragged them away from the bittersweet pleasure of exploring each other's bodies.

Kate looked at the two figures waiting beside the vehicles, and her paddling slowed. Once they landed, this idyll would be over.

Jordan scanned the shore for a docking point. "I need to go back to our local base for an hour or so, catch up on operations."

Silently, Kate picked up her pace again. For most of this trip she'd been living outside her comfort zone physically and mentally, but as she stared at the placid river and the wild and beautiful landscape for the last time, she experienced a sense of loss so acute it brought tears to her eyes.

"So how does it feel to be back in civilization?" Mike joked as he and Dillon helped them drag the canoe onto the bank.

Kate looked around, but saw only a cluster of tiny houses and one shop, almost smothered in goods. The brochure racks proclaimed it a visitor center; the displays of fruit and vegetables, a grocery store; and the bucket of brooms and mops, a hardware store. "I'm giddy with excitement," she said.

Dillon had already made a friend of

Doug, the bushman transporting their canoes. She listened with amusement as the boy talked a mile a minute about his adventures, then looked at her lover, to share the joke. But, intent on unloading, Jordan didn't glance up. So she said her farewells to Dillon and Mike. Dillon gave her a big hug. "Will I see you again, Kate?"

"Yes," answered Jordan, "you will."

"I hope so," she said, unwilling to make promises she might not be able to keep. Who knew how long she and Jordan would last?

Mike looked from Jordan to her, and gave Kate a hug. "I hope so, too." He shook Jordan's hand. "You'll be getting a wedding invitation in the near future."

Jordan grinned. "I'm glad." He picked Dillon up and gave him a bear hug. "Next time we go on a fishing trip, bring your dad...I need bait."

"Yeah, yeah," said Mike, "you just want a medic on hand in case you have any more fainting spells, princess."

Jordan shot a glance at Doug, then lowered his voice. "Didn't we make an arrangement about that?"

"We did, but it wasn't time specific. I figured twenty-four hours."

"Mike," Jordan said in alarm, "we need to talk."

Mike winked. "Have your people call my people. Goodbye, Kate."

After they'd left, Kate finished unloading the gear. Her fingers touched Jordan's as she handed over her life jacket, and this time their eyes met. His answering smile was as brief and polite as a stranger's. Kate dropped her arm and took an instinctive step backward.

Jordan slammed the boot. "I'll see you back in Auckland."

"Thanks for the trip," she answered formally.

He looked at her sharply. "It's not over yet."

Kate nodded to Doug. "Nice to meet you, too."

Jordan handed the man some coins. "Nip into the store and get us some chocolate, will you, mate?"

Kate was standing by her car, burrowing for her keys, when she found herself spun around and thoroughly kissed. "Listen, prickles, in case you've forgotten, you've got to broadcast that broken engagement before we go public. Doug doesn't say much, but what he does say will be in Auckland before we are. I'll call you as soon as I get back."

Kate nodded, feeling like a fool. She'd been so wrapped up in the romance she hadn't thought about repercussions in the real world. She'd told Peter she'd maintain their phony engagement for another three weeks.

Before she could discuss it with Jordan, Doug came back and the two men left. Deep in thought, Kate turned on her cell phone and waded through twenty messages. One was from Danny.

"Hey, Katie, had dinner with Dad. I was

calling to give you an update, but it's probably better to do it in person, so I'll leave it until we get home. See you in a week." She played it again, trying to pick up some clue from her brother's pitch, but static made it impossible.

If Kate needed another reminder that she was back in the real world, arriving in Auckland at rush hour provided it. Her apartment was cold, the mail neatly stacked on her hall table by a kind neighbor.

She'd forgotten to empty a vase of flowers, and the familiar smell of vegetative decay made her chuckle—a chuckle that caught in her throat when she spotted her father's handwriting on one of the letters.

Normally she returned his correspondence unopened, but she hesitated, remembering her promise to Mike. Without giving herself time to chicken out, she ripped open the envelope. *"My darling girl…"*

Kate closed her eyes, feeling a rush of emotion. When she was little, Cliff had always called her that. But before she could read any further the doorbell rang.

Peter was standing on the doorstep.

"Pete," she said, surprised, "How did you know I was back?"

"I called your office, and they said you'd rung in."

"I guess you've come for the ring."

He followed her into the hall. "Actually, the decision on my shareholding has been postponed an extra week. I need you to go along with the engagement for another month."

Kate's phone started ringing. She ignored it. "I was going to give you a call about that. Something's happened that makes it difficult."

Jordan's voice kicked in on the answering machine. "Hey, babe, I have to go to Queenstown for a couple of days, but keep Monday night free. We might even try sex in a bed. How about wear—"

Mortified, Kate dived for the off button, then turned to see Peter's face suffused with color. "Surely, you're not so stupid as to fall for one of Jordan King's lines?"

Her embarrassment turned to defiance. "Why not? I was stupid enough to believe all yours. How do you think I felt when I discovered you'd crawled to Jordan, apologizing for me?"

"*He* told you, I suppose."

Kate looked at him steadily. "Did he lie, Peter?"

He couldn't hold her gaze. "Damn it, I thought my job was on the line."

"I don't want to trade recriminations with you," she said. "Let's just accept that a marriage between us would never have lasted."

"It would have lasted a damn sight longer than you and King will!" He ran a scathing eye over her bedraggled appearance. "You might have held his interest in the wilderness, but you won't last five minutes against real competition."

Kate went to the front door and held it wide. "Goodbye, Peter."

"Damn it, Kate, I hope you're going to honor our deal." He seemed to realize he was shooting himself in the foot, because he was all conciliation again. "I'm sorry, but you can see why I'm upset."

"Yes," she said tiredly. "You want that shareholding and you think being engaged to me will get it for you. Image is everything, isn't it, Peter? For old times' sake, I'll give you a week. Use it whichever way you think best. But I won't live a lie any longer than that."

CHAPTER NINETEEN

"WHERE THE HELL have you been?" Jordan demanded into his car phone. "I'm too busy to be worried about you."

Hearing the annoyance in his tone made him even more irritated. His conflict wasn't with Kate; it was with himself.

When she didn't answer, Jordan sighed. "I'm sorry." Realizing the speedometer had crept well over the speed limit, he slowed down. "I've been imagining you in some ditch between here and Whanganui."

He'd been running from one crisis to another ever since he'd left her. Seemed like Triton had a thousand operational problems needing his attention. And then there was that heli-skiing operator in

Queenstown who was thinking of selling. Did Triton want first option?

Hell, yes! Christian had been drooling over the business for two years. He and Luke were satisfied; it only needed Jordan to fly down and make an operational assessment, and quickly, before competitors got wind of the deal. Part of him was glad to go. A few days apart from Kate would give him a chance to get his head straight.

"I'm fine," she said over the phone.

Immediately, Jordan started looking for the nearest exit off the motorway. "You've been crying."

"Peter heard your message…."

"It was bad," he stated quietly.

"Awful, but I don't want to talk about it." There was a catch in her voice, quickly controlled. "I promised Peter I'd give him a week before we officially break off our engagement, so you and I need to keep our relationship secret."

"You don't want to go back to him, do you?"

There was a long and terrible pause. "Would you want me to?"

Jordan made himself say the right thing. "It's not about what I want." There was another gut-wrenching silence. "Don't you dare," he said vehemently. So much for self-sacrifice.

Her laughter put his fears to rest. "I won't. Incidentally, where are you?"

"Driving to the airport." Ahead, an exit sign appeared, and Jordan wavered. It flashed by as he made his decision. She was okay now, and this deal was too important. He'd spent the long drive back to Auckland thinking about what she'd said in the tent, and come to the conclusion that they'd reached the best possible arrangement. But he couldn't stop himself saying, "Miss me."

"Have a good trip," she said softly.

Jordan hesitated. To hell with it. "I'll miss you," he said. But Kate had already hung up.

TRENDY, RAUCOUS AND brightly lit, the Bar wasn't an ideal venue for an assignation with your secret lover—except on Monday nights. Hank, the owner, was American, and after the NFL football season back home, he reran key games, hoping for converts. Instead, he effectively cleared the place out.

Having spent some time in the States and been educated in the rules of the game, Jordan enjoyed the NFL and often kept poor Hank company over a Budweiser while they relived the highlights. But not tonight. Tonight he was meeting Kate.

He couldn't believe how nervous he was. Nervous enough to be thirty minutes early. Nervous enough to be checking his watch every ten minutes and his text messages every five.

Jordan took another gulp of his beer and realized he'd finished his second. He needed to slow down, get a grip on himself, peel his eyes off the entrance. He felt like a goddamn Labrador waiting for its owner to come home. *So much for using our separation to regain some perspective.*

Deliberately, he looked at the screen and watched a couple of plays, but his attention swung back to the door as soon as he heard it open. And his heart sank.

A gaggle of laughing, inebriated women poured in, led by a sexy blonde with a bridal veil askew on her glossy head.

"I thought you said this place was wild, Imogen," complained a baby-faced brunette who was using the door for support. "Plen'ee of talent."

"It *usually* is." Disconsolately the blonde scanned the bar, and Jordan slunk back into the booth. *Please don't see me. Please don't—* A squeal rent the air. "It's okay, girls, Jord's here."

Half-a-dozen pairs of stilettos clip-clopped across the floor, sounding like a herd of My Little Ponies. With no help for it, Jordan smiled and stood up. "Immy, hey, you're on your hen night."

"Yep, so make the most of your last opportunity to kiss the bride," she said, and laid a smacker on him that tasted of four hours of serious drinking.

Jordan managed to keep his mouth closed despite her best efforts, and Immy stumbled back, clearly puzzled. "Oops. Guess I'm drunker than I thought. Thanks for keepin' me honest, hon."

Over Immy's shoulder, Jordan's gaze met Kate's. For a split second he thought he saw hurt in her eyes, but then she waved. His heart started pounding; his palms got clammy.

"So…" said Immy, "this is my friend Sarah an' Tanya an' Melanie an' Ruth an—"

"Kate." Jordan reached through the press of women and pulled her to his side. He bent his head to kiss her, but she averted her face so his lips brushed her cheek. He'd forgotten they were playing it cool in public.

"Hi, Kate," squealed Immy, full of alcohol-induced joy. The others didn't look so pleased. "You must be Jord's new—"

"Friend." Kate loosened his grip. "We're just friends." Jordan slid his hand down the curve of her sweet ass, and she jumped and lifted it back around her waist.

"Oh, another ex," said Immy. "I'm one of those, too. Nice, isn't it, how you stay friends with him? He's always been good like that."

Kate blinked and Jordan intervened. "Well, Immy, you and the girls have a great time. I'm—"

"So if it's not a date, you won't mind if we join you." Giggling, Immy shoved him in the direction of the bar. "We're drinking champagne."

"Imogen, I'm happy to buy you all drinks, but Kate and I are—"

"Don't be a spoilsport," Kate interrupted. She turned to Immy. "So there must be an ex-girlfriends club I can join?"

"Red…" he warned.

"I'm more interested in the future girlfriends club." The baby-faced brunette sent him a smoldering look, but her smudged mascara reduced it to charcoal. It was Kate's turn to blanch.

Giving her shoulder a reassuring squeeze, Jordan retreated to the bar and ordered champagne cocktails. While he waited, he stared ruefully at his lover. This wasn't the evening he'd planned. Drinks, a candlelit dinner, seduction in a big bed…romance, not farce.

And in his heated fantasies of the past couple of days, Kate hadn't been wearing a conservative navy business suit and sensible heels…though she was still the sexiest woman in the room, in control and classy.

She'd kept her curls, he noticed with satisfaction, though they looked a little regimented. The first thing he was going to do when he got her alone was tousle her hair. The second would be to strip off that corporate uniform and uncover more of her sinful underwear.

He chuckled, finally understanding why women liked men in uniforms. It was all about corruption.

As if sensing his scrutiny, Kate looked at him, and Jordan's body hardened as he saw the same fierce hunger for contact in her. He threw a smoldering glance of his own.

Kate lost her place in the conversation.

"Your eyes have glazed over," said Immy. "Let's sit down." Kate found herself shunted into a booth and trapped in a cloud of soft perfume and hard liquor fumes. The other women remained standing, watching Jordan's butt as he reached into the back pocket of his jeans for his wallet.

"Money *and* muscle," murmured a petite redhead with an hourglass figure. "Yum, yum."

"Mind if I hit on him?" said the brunette with panda eyes.

Kate opened her mouth to snap, "Yes, I bloody do," before realizing the woman was talking to Imogen.

"Sweetie, you are so out of your league," the bride-to-be said, "but sure, give it your best shot."

"I wonder how he feels about redheads," said the redhead. She looked at Kate and brightened. Kate dug her nails into her palms.

"Come on," said one of the others. "Let's give them some competition."

"But we're married."

"We can still flirt with a good-looking man, can't we?"

Kate watched them surround Jordan and jostle for his attention. Luckily, he was head and shoulders taller, or he'd be drowning in them.

"Is it always like this?" she asked.

Immy paused in her wobbly reapplication of lipstick. "Jeez, where did you two date…Siberia?"

"Close."

Immy dropped her lipstick back into her evening purse. "You still love him, don't you?"

Not so drunk, then. Kate gave a non-committal shrug.

"What those girls don't realize—and you and I know—is how hard it is being with a guy like that. Male or female, everyone wants a piece of him. But see how he keeps it light?"

Laughing, Jordan fended off the brunette when she tried to whisper in his ear, and adroitly repositioned himself between the married women while he handed out cocktails. "An easy grin here, a joke there," said Immy, "never engaging too deeply." Her pretty mouth twisted. "And that ends up being the problem—it doesn't mean anything with you, either. Not beyond a good time. At least you managed to work that one out early. 'Course, it takes a lot longer to get over him, but, hey, I'm living proof." Immy held out her ruby engagement ring. "Gorgeous, huh? And David loves me like he should. Anyway, I gotta pee."

Left alone, Kate stared forlornly at the big screen. The Steelers were playing. She watched a wide receiver field a punt, trying not to feel like a kid whose party balloons had popped early.

You might have held his interest in the

wilderness, but you won't last five minutes against real competition.

This was the real world. Jordan had been calling every night he'd been away, and fool that she was, Kate had allowed herself to hope.

She started as Jordan dumped some drinks on the table, grabbed her arm and said, "Let's get the hell out of here while Immy's gone."

"Isn't that rude?"

He hauled her to her feet. "She'll forgive me when she hears how much money I left at the bar."

"Buying yourself out of trouble?" Kate realized she was angry the moment the words left her mouth.

Jordan simply grinned. "I'd buy her a honeymoon in Europe to get you alone right now. You can bitch at me outside."

He slid them through Immy's crowd of resistant friends like an eel through waterweed, and they were outside breathing cold air in less than thirty seconds. They stared at each other a minute. "Well," Kate said lightly, "that was interesting."

"God, I missed you."

She felt a queer lump in her throat. "I'm starting to think that this isn't a good—"

Jordan kissed her and Kate's reserve crumbled. Heedless of passersby, she wrapped her arms around his neck.

When the kiss ended they were both breathing hard. "Screw dinner," he said. "Come home with me. It's my birthday—" he nipped the lobe of her ear "—and you're the only present I want."

"Now that's definitely a line!"

Smugly, Jordan took out his driver's license and showed her the date. A warm glow spread through Kate. "Don't your family and friends want to celebrate with you?"

"I put them off…don't worry, I didn't say why. It's your call when we come out of the closet. In the meantime…" He pulled her down the narrow alleyway adjoining the Bar.

This kiss left them panting. "Where's your car?" Kate demanded in a voice not her own.

"In the car park across the road." His voice was as husky as hers.

She kissed him again. "Mine's closer." Grabbing his hand, she started running down the street. Jordan didn't laugh. At her Fiat she caught his hair and tugged him into another kiss, hotter, wilder, but he paid her back once they were in the car, his hands sliding under her skirt, driving her insane with so much but no more.

Kate wrenched her mouth from his, dragged her hands out of his jeans and stumbled out of the car, tossing the keys to him. "You drive, my brain's scrambled."

With an unsteady chuckle he took her place at the wheel; deliberately, she got in the backseat. "I know what you can do with one hand," she said hoarsely, and Jordan laughed as he revved the engine.

Kate gripped the seat in front to stop herself from falling sideways as he swung the vehicle into traffic and sped down the road. When his cell phone rang, Jordan dragged it out of his unbuttoned shirt, glanced at the number and answered. "Hey, Christian."

In the rearview mirror his gaze, languorous with heat, met Kate's, and she caught her breath. "Yeah, as it happens I'm heading home now, should be there in ten. Why are those figures so urgent? Uh-huh, well, I'll call you as soon as I get there." He was frowning slightly as he hung up, and Kate stopped straightening her clothes.

"Please don't tell me you have to work."

"Ten minutes tops, then I'm all yours," he reassured her. A wicked smile curved his mouth. "Show me your underwear."

"Not while you're driving," she said primly, and instead tortured him with word pictures. By the time they stood at his front door it took both of them to steady the key.

"At last." Lips locked in an open-mouthed kiss, Kate grabbed his shirt and dragged him through the door, while Jordan fumbled for the zipper on her skirt.

The lights came on and a chorus of voices yelled, "Surprise!"

CHAPTER TWENTY

"I DON'T SEE WHY YOU couldn't have held the damn party at your house." Jordan stood on his deck with Christian and Luke and stared moodily down at the barbecue. He was nursing a beer and a sense of grievance.

Christian turned the steaks and blue flames shot through the grill. "You don't think I was going to trash *my* place, did you?"

He was ruining those steaks, Jordan noticed, but figured his friends and family deserved to eat tough meat. Throwing him a surprise birthday party and not telling him…

It was too damn cold to barbecue, anyway, but as the autumn chill kept everyone else inside, he should be grateful for the respite from the ribbing he'd endured over the past hour. Scowling, he finished his beer and reached for another.

"You can't blame us for this." Luke's tone was as reasonable as Christian's. As though Jordan couldn't sense their unholy mirth. "You told us nothing happened on the river trip."

Jordan switched on the pool lights and the water came into sharp relief, glowing an eerie blue. With better visibility, the steaks looked even worse. "She wanted to keep it quiet for a week because of a promise she made to her ex."

Through the French doors, Kate sat primly on the couch talking to his mother, and trying to act as if she hadn't been caught with her tongue down his throat.

And doing a damn fine job. He hadn't wanted to leave her, but his mother had shoved a package of meat into his hands and sent him outside.

Actually, Kate had handled the whole situation much better than he had. But then, he reflected, she hadn't been the one trying to hide a hard-on. "Give me that."

He confiscated the tongs from Christian and tried to salvage the steak. The sausages, wizened and black, were beyond help.

Out of the corner of his eye he saw his friends exchange the look. Okay, there was another reason it suited him to keep their relationship quiet a little longer. "Don't read too much into this," he warned. He was coming around to love, but commitment? No way was he ready for that.

"Kiss kiss, bang bang?" Christian's blue eyes were full of mischief.

"Will you quit with the gun thing? I'm handling it." Irritated, Jordan returned his gaze to Kate. He wondered if she'd wait until he was ready. "Hold on a minute... is grubby Uncle Burt hitting on her?" Incredulous, he watched his geriatric relative kiss Kate's fingers by way of introduction.

"Doesn't he know where that hand's been?" said Luke. For a moment there was absolute silence, then they all started to laugh, harder and harder until they had to pull up deck chairs and sit down.

"Oh, God." Jordan wiped the last tears from his eyes and returned to the barbecue. "I needed that."

"The two of you frozen like possums caught in the headlights, it'll go down as one of my favorite memories." Christian started laughing again.

"So when's the wedding?" Luke asked innocently.

"That's fighting talk."

"So you don't love her?" said Christian.

It was as if they had him in a headlock and were pummeling the crap out of him. "You've got to keep some space around you," Jordan hedged, "breathing room."

Christian shrugged. "Sounds lonely to me."

"Not lonely," said Luke, "safe...I can understand that."

"So can I—in you." Christian took a

swig of his soda. "But why is our adventurer suddenly desperate to play it safe?"

Jordan narrowed his eyes. "You *want* to wear a bridesmaid dress to my wedding, asshole?" he said softly.

His friend paled. "Shit, I forgot about that." He threw an arm around Jordan's shoulders. "You take your time, mate. Don't rush into anything."

"Huh," said Jordan, slightly mollified.

"He won't hold me to it," Christian stage-whispered to Luke. "He'll be too happy."

Disgusted, Jordan shoved him away and returned to barbecuing.

"If you think that, you're even more deluded than Jordan," said Luke dryly. "Besides, you think I'd let you welsh?"

Christian hid his face in his hands. "Does Armani do bridesmaid stuff?"

"I'll be lobbying for pink gingham," said Luke, "in keeping with your country origins an' all."

"You bastard," Christian said appreciatively, sinking on a deck chair.

Though it killed him to miss a chance to torture Christian, Jordan maintained a dignified silence.

Luke slapped him on the back. "I'm going inside to talk to Kate."

Jordan resisted until he heard the door open and the music grow louder. "Luke?"

Luke turned around and his friend's expression nearly changed Jordan's mind. Bloody know-it-all.

"Yeah, Jord?"

Sighing, he said softly, "Like her, will you?"

ONLY HALF LISTENING to Uncle Burt, Kate watched Jordan's friend zigzag through the crowd, holding a wine bottle and a can of beer. A former athlete, apparently. But she'd seen the three men laughing together, obviously treating this whole humiliating experience as a great joke.

When she'd turned to flee, Jordan had clamped her to his side and said, "The only way out is through." Easy for him to say; he'd probably been discovered in flagrante delicto several times in his adult life.

"Hi, I'm Luke," said the dark-haired man. "One of Jordan's partners. I've come to stop Uncle Burt from stealing a match on his great-nephew."

The old man laughed delightedly. "Well, you can't blame a guy for trying." He allowed Luke to help him up from the couch, bowed, and moved on.

Luke sat, refilled her glass, then tipped his beer to it. "Cheers." Keen gray eyes assessed her.

"Say it," she invited. "Everyone else has. 'You're not his type.'"

"Do you always fish for compliments?"

Reluctantly, she smiled. "Thank you. I was starting to get a complex." He smiled back and got even more handsome. "So," she said politely, "what do you do in the Triton partnership?"

"At the moment? Not much. I'm trying to set up a camp for disadvantaged kids in

Beacon Bay." He watched her. "Which is proving a lot harder than we thought."

"Not helped by my columns, I've been told."

His mouth tightened. "Or Jordan's infuriating tendency to wave red rags at bulls."

"Ouch. Me being the bull."

"No, that was what you wrote."

Ouch again. Kate's stomach swooped as she had an awful thought. "I might have just got the camp into more trouble. I fully intend to run a positive column, but if everyone knows Jordan and I are... together, it's hardly going to be perceived as impartial." Kate was suddenly very tired. "This goes from bad to worse."

"That is a problem," agreed Luke. "But there's got to be a way around it."

Jordan came inside carrying a plate of blackened meat, and was waylaid by a stunning brunette. He kissed her with enthusiasm.

Luke followed Kate's gaze. "That's

Kezia, married to Christian, our other partner."

She forced a laugh. "Is this where his best friend tells me to trust him?"

"No," he said, surprising her, "that's his job."

Their eyes met. "I disliked you before you came over, you know," Kate said gruffly. "I saw you all laughing."

"We were laughing at Jord, not you," said another beautiful man with a deep voice, holding an even more beautiful baby. He took the other side of the couch. "Because he's a goner and doesn't know it yet." He held out a hand. "I'm Christian and this is Maddie, who won't go to bed."

Kate shook his hand. "Please don't read too much into our relationship," she said earnestly, then realized she was still gripping Christian's hand, and dropped it.

To hide her embarrassment, she cooed at the baby, who stared back with wide eyes, the same penetrating blue as her father's. "To be honest, he's not the only one dating against type. I'm sure it will burn itself out soon…I mean it has to, right?" She took a gulp of wine, to stop the spill of words. Christian held out the baby. Gratefully, Kate took her and laid her cheek against Maddie's downy black hair. The baby gurgled and gummed her face.

"Two people used to control out of control with each other," murmured Christian. "I've been there myself."

He glanced over at his wife, who was still talking to Jordan.

Oh, God, what I wouldn't give for Jordan to look at me like that, Kate thought. She turned her head to see Jordan staring at her with a look of total dismay.

"DEEP BREATHS," Kezia suggested.

Turning his back on the tableau, Jordan took a deep draft of his beer instead, but the vision of Kate, cheek to cheek with the baby, haunted him.

This was all happening too fast. He

took another swig of his drink. "Beer isn't working. I'm going to have to move on to tequila."

"Tequila isn't the answer in matters of the heart," said Kez piously, and Jordan recalled the first time he and Luke had met her—drowning her sorrows after fighting with Christian.

"You're right." He grabbed her arm and headed for the drinks cabinet. "It was whiskey you drank, wasn't it?"

"Wait a minute, why do I have to come?" she protested.

"Because I don't want you sneaking off and changing sides. It's enough that my two best friends have turned traitor."

Her eyes sparkled. "Your sisters think she's exactly the sort of woman to keep you in order."

"That's right," he complained bitterly, "twist the knife."

He unscrewed the cap on a bottle of Chivas Regal and splashed the amber liquid into a crystal tumbler. Kezia stopped him as he lifted the glass. "You don't have to marry her if you don't want to," she reminded him gently.

"That's the problem." Jordan threw back the drink, relishing the burn down his throat. "I think I do want to."

He turned back to see Kate grab her coat and head for the door.

He came up behind her as she opened it, and leaned against it. "You can't go."

"Watch me."

Jordan pulled her into his study and closed the door.

"Talk to me."

"You were looking at me like a tooth that needs pulling." Kate had been kidding herself that a short romance was better than none. In reality it was like living on death row.

"I think I'm in love with you."

If anything, she felt more hurt. "And you don't want to be."

"It's not something I'd choose right now," he admitted.

Kate had hoped he'd deny it, and despised herself for her weakness. He'd never pretended, never made promises, never said or done anything to make her believe he was a commitment kind of guy.

"Well, let me take the choice out of your hands. Goodbye."

"You're dumping me?" His incredulity made Kate mad. His disappointment wasn't about love; it was about ego.

"Yes. I could have handled light, I could have handled 'no strings,' but I'm damned if I'll accept horror-struck."

"Kate, I'm being cautious because I don't want to hurt you."

"No, Jordan, you're being cautious because *you* don't want to get hurt. Step aside."

"Give me time," he said desperately, "to get it straight in my head."

"I need you to love me the way I love you, from the heart. If you're not prepared to do that, then step aside."

He stepped aside.

"EVERYTHING OKAY?"

Jordan looked up from the couch to see his two friends at the study door, music pouring in with them. He'd forgotten he still had guests.

He raised an imaginary gun to his head and pulled the trigger. "Laugh," he invited, "I know you want to."

"I want to," admitted Christian, "but I can't because I know how bad it feels."

Jordan looked up at Luke, who shrugged. "Frankly, I never thought it was funny."

"You have to." Jordan got mad. "I need you guys to make light of it, to tell me I'm better off without a bossy redhead, that I'm not ready."

"Trouble is," interrupted Luke, "if you don't believe it, we can't make you."

"This is your fault." Jordan stabbed a finger toward Christian's chest. "You and that damn gun prophecy of yours, worming its way into my subconscious, screwing with my mind."

"That's right, buddy," said Christian soothingly, "let it all out."

He threw his hands up in disgust. "What does the woman want…? I *told* her I loved her."

"Did you sound this happy about it?" Luke asked carefully.

"I said the timing wasn't great. What, should I have I lied?"

Christian exchanged a look with Luke. "You know what surprises me?"

"Yeah, that *Kate* didn't use the gun," Luke answered. "Without sounding unsympathetic, Jordan, how is this breakup going to affect Saturday's column?"

"KATE." Her editor stuck his head in the door. "I've been talking to Jordan King. He said you won't return his calls."

The column. In the end, that was all Jordan cared about. Kate was trying to be fair, knowing the camp was so much more important than her broken heart.

"It's okay," she said, through the agony. "Everything is under control."

Unconvinced, Henry came in. "King's concerned about your credibility if you print a column and readers find out you have a personal relationship. He's suggesting you don't write anything. He'll find another fix for his reputation."

"What he's really worried about," Kate said bitterly, "is that I'm going to rip him apart in the column because we *ended* that personal relationship. It's a ploy to shut me down." She told her editor what her plan was and, satisfied, he went away.

Alone, Kate stared blindly at the words on her screen. She didn't think Jordan could hurt her any more than he had the night of the party. She'd been wrong.

THERE WAS ONLY ONE recourse left to him and Jordan took it. He couldn't let Kate print that column; the gossip mill was already circulating stories of how the two of them had been "surprised" at his birthday party. Sooner or later a tabloid would pick up the story.

Good or bad, Kate's credibility would suffer. And he'd made her suffer enough. Any hope of salvaging his own reputation was long gone. All social services and the anti-camp brigade would see was Jordan embroiled in yet another scandal—corrupting a respected journalist.

Two days before Kate's column was due to be printed, he walked into the spartan office of social services and shook hands with the director in charge of approving the camp, the one who'd raised concerns about Jordan's involvement.

"A real pleasure to meet you," Keith Forsyth greeted him warmly. "Sit down, sit down."

Puzzled, Jordan took a seat. He'd expected reserve, even hostility. "You *do* know who I am?"

"Very funny, yes, very good." Keith smiled at him across the desk. "So—" the man raised his grizzled brows "—what can I do for you?"

Jordan handed over the documents he'd prepared. "Here's my resignation as camp trustee," he said. "The second document is a report outlining how I intend to separate myself from the business I own with the two other camp trustees, Luke Carter and Christian Kelly. Neither of my business partners know yet, so I'd appreciate it if you kept this confidential. I want to make sure these will address your concerns before I tell them." Jordan sat back in his chair. Kate had been right all along; this was *his* mess to fix.

Keith was frowning and Jordan's tired brain searched for the angles he must have missed. Between making this decision, meeting secretly with Triton's accountant and missing Kate, he hadn't slept in three days.

"Well, I have to say—" Keith shook his head "—I'm very disappointed. I hope you'll reconsider."

"You *don't* know who I am, do you?" Jordan said at last. "The guy with the messy private life who needs to step back from the camp or you'll—rightly—withdraw your support."

Keith looked at him for a long moment. "I assume you haven't seen an advance copy of Kate Brogan's column? She was kind enough to send me one."

That hurt. Jordan hadn't expected positive, but he hadn't expected vindictive, either. He kept his tone neutral. "May I see it?"

It's impossible for me to be impartial about Jordan King so I'm not even going to try. After reading the first line, Jordan braced himself. *Turns out a lot of other people aren't impartial about him, either.*

He pushed the column across the desk. "Maybe I don't want to read it, after all."

Keith pushed it back. "Keep going."

What follows are testimonials from all the people Jordan King has helped over the years...a bunch of naughty boys and ratbags who have grown up to be (mostly) responsible and law-abiding citizens. I leave you to make up your own mind about what kind of man Jordan King really is.

Jordan became very still.

Jordan King collects strays, Christian wrote. *He always has. In his own pushy way, he 'adopted' Luke and me, two bad boys from dysfunctional families, when we were all at university together, and took us home to his family. We've never left.*

In watching Jordan support his large family through the tough times following his father's death, wrote Luke, *I saw the kind of man I wanted to be. In a real sense, he emotionally prepared Christian and me to start Camp Chance.*

Keith shoved a box of tissues across the desk, and Jordan realized he was crying. "I'm sorry," he said, wiping his eyes.

"I teared up myself," Keith said, and ripped up the documents Jordan had given him.

Back in his car, Jordan rang Kate's

editor and waited until the man forced her to take the phone. "I've just seen an advanced copy of your column and I…" The words caught in his throat. "Kate, I love you. I've been fighting it because I'm so damn scared of how I feel about you. I choked and I'm sorry."

"You know what gets me most?" she asked quietly. "You thought I'd let my personal disappointment get in the way of doing the right thing."

"Only because I knew how much I'd hurt you."

"That hurt me more," she said. "If you don't really know me, then I can't trust your feelings for me."

"Give me another chance, Kate, please. This is real, you know it is."

"I want to believe you," she said, "but I can't. Goodbye, Jordan." And she hung up.

CHAPTER TWENTY-ONE

"WE'VE BEEN LOOKING for you."

Jordan opened his eyes and squinted against the afternoon sun. Christian and Luke stood gazing down at him, two slicks in designer suits and sunglasses.

He should have known his friends would track him down. But then it wasn't rocket science. Whenever he had a thorny problem to think through, he would cross the road from their offices and find a bench among the trees in Victoria Park.

"Shit. I forgot that meeting," he said, registering the significance of their attire.

"We managed without you," said Luke. "What's wrong?"

"Kate won't take me back." He'd returned to work because he couldn't stand to be alone with his thoughts, but the office chatter was worse. His life had fallen apart; he didn't give a damn that Triton had successfully signed the Queenstown deal.

His friends sat on either side of him.

"I've been tearing my hair out for the past hour," Jordan said, "trying to think of a way to prove I'm ready for love, marriage, the whole kit and caboodle. Nothing. I don't know how to fix this."

"Give up, then," advised Luke.

"That's it?" Jordan snapped. "That's your advice?"

"Luke's right," said Christian. "It's way too hard."

"What the hell are you talking about?" he roared. He got up and started pacing.

"Make him mad," said Luke. "Always works."

Jordan ignored them. "A gesture she can't argue with...something that removes every doubt about my ability to make a commitment. A gesture as big-hearted as hers." He glanced up. "Speaking of which, I read what you wrote about me and I just wanted to say—"

Christian turned to Luke. "It's so great being with the guys, isn't it? You don't have to do postmortems on icky stuff like feelings."

"You've got that right," said Luke.

Jordan grinned. "I knew you'd be embarrassed." His spirits lifted, and he felt hopeful again. "Okay, I'll leave you two to talk manly stuff—like Christian's bridesmaid dress." He started down the path.

"Are you that confident of getting the girl?" Luke called curiously.

"No," replied Jordan. "The only thing I know for sure is that I'm prepared to die trying."

"THESE ARE FOR YOU." Kate's secretary walked in with a long elegant box, lavish with red ribbons, and shook her head. The office was strewn with empty coffee cups and papers. "What time did you get here this morning?"

"Five," Kate admitted, rubbing her eyes. Work was normally a panacea, but this time it was failing her. Still, it had to be better than tossing and turning.

"Where shall I put these?"

"I'll take them." Did Jordan honestly think he could change her mind with flowers? Depressed, Kate pushed the box aside and kept working, but it was harder to ignore the gilt-edged card. She resisted for another thirty minutes, then gave up and opened it.

Remember the conversation around the campfire when I said I'd never met the right woman and Mike said, "Maybe you were never the right man?" We were both right.

Intrigued now, she undid the ribbons on the box and lifted the last of the tissue paper. For a moment Kate stared blankly at the contents, then started to tremble. The box fell, spilling the contents across the navy carpet.

Dropping to her knees, she scrambled to capture the loose strands and returned them to the skein of hair, which lay like spun gold half in, half out of the box. It was like trying to pick up fairy dust.

She rocked back on her heels and covered her face with her hands. "You cut your hair," she whispered, and burst into tears.

Through her trembling fingers she caught sight of another card, still lying in the box.

You're the right woman, Kate. I'm ready to be the right man.

SHIRTLESS, JORDAN WAS attracting a lot of female interest, poolside at the Cook Islands Beach Resort.

Returning from an afternoon with her father, Kate stood for a moment in the hotel's tropical gardens, lush with palms, exotic blooms and sweet-smelling gardenias, admiring her new husband and smiling as every woman who caught sight of him did a double take. *Sorry, ladies, he's all mine.*

Oblivious to the attention, Jordan stretched out in a deck chair with a drink and a book he wasn't really reading. He was waiting for her. Kate could tell by the way he glanced up every time someone came through the hotel lobby.

With his short blond hair disheveled from a swim, and a five o'clock shadow closer to midnight, he looked rugged and as sexy as hell. He kept telling her she was shallow because she was insisting he grow his hair back; she was happy to admit it.

On impulse, Kate swapped the red hibiscus Fay had given her to her left ear, reclaiming her single status, and stepped out from behind the buttercup tree. Even after a week of marriage, meeting those blue eyes could still make her blush. He had a wicked ability to conjure erotic images with one intense glance.

This time Kate returned a slow, sensual smile, then her gaze swept provocatively over his half-naked body. Amused, Jordan leaned back in the deck chair and returned her scrutiny—and then some.

Kate crossed her arms to make sure he didn't miss the cleavage under her pretty green dress.

Jordan's eyes lifted to meet hers and his answer was most definitely yes.

Kate started to laugh. "Let me think about it," she called.

Jordan got up. Oh boy, she knew what *that* look meant.

But she stood her ground. Her new husband was going to have to learn he couldn't daunt her. He stopped a foot away. "Wife," he said lovingly, "you just reminded me of one lesson I've been meaning to teach you."

"What's that, big guy?" Kate teased, knowing she was safe in this crowd.

She gasped as Jordan picked her up and threw her over his shoulder. "I'm going to teach you, Mrs. King, why little girls shouldn't tease big boys," he said, and carried her, laughing and breathless, to bed.

* * * * *

Turn the page for a sneak peek at
Father Material *by Kimberly Van Meter*
available from Mills & Boon® Superromance
in May 2008!

Father Material

by

Kimberly Van Meter

THE HIGH SUN glinted off the river, its smooth surface broken only by the frothy whitecaps that churned against the rocks hidden beneath, and Natalie Simmons's step faltered as she surveyed its awesome power. Her gaze traveled along the limestone and shale canyon cliffs the river was nestled between and the breath was stolen from her chest.

Holy Mother, she'd never felt so small.

"Amazing, isn't it?" a man with blond hair and a lazy smile asked as he approached, reading her expression. She recovered with a shy nod, accepting his outstretched hand for a quick shake. "It never fails to get me right here every time," he said, knocking on his chest for emphasis. He grinned broadly, showcasing nice, white even teeth that surely made his dentist proud and she found herself smiling back, though she'd never been what could be deemed a flirt by any stretch of the imagination. "Name's Evan. I'll be your guide. What's yours?"

"N-Natalie," she warbled around the dust in her throat. He chuckled as if she weren't the first one to suffer from too much nature all at once and she tried again. "Natalie Simmons."

"Well, Natalie, welcome to Moab. Just sit tight and someone will come to put your stuff with the others. We should be ready to shove off soon."

It was on the tip of her tongue to ask if another bus was coming, as she still hadn't seen Dan anywhere, but Evan the River Guide Guy was gone before she could put the words together. She started toward the cluster of people Evan had pointed to, all the while keeping an eye out for the one person she'd made this trip for.

She couldn't wait to see the look on Dan's face when he saw her. The urge to giggle almost relieved the tightness in her lungs but she contented herself with a secret smile, knowing everything was going to work out.

Another five minutes crawled by and Natalie slapped her thigh in mild annoyance—he was late. Dan was always late.

They used to joke he'd be the type to skid in on one foot to the chapel. She'd, of course, threatened him with bodily harm if he did that on their wedding day and they'd laughed. She swallowed and flinched at the sharp pain that followed but managed to keep her eyes dry. She fingered the pendant around her neck for strength. A gift from her oldest sister before she left for the Peace Corps many years ago, the pendant served to remind her she wasn't here to cry. She'd done enough of that the first month after Dan had left. Now was the time to be proactive. If Dan was going river-rafting, by damn, so was she. She'd show him there were more dimensions to Natalie Simmons than he ever dreamed. Boring, indeed. Predictable, watch this. She was practically a goddamn daredevil, she thought glancing at the river again as if it were a coconspirator, and not the subject of her nightmares a full week running prior to her flight date.

Squaring her shoulders, she jerked at the suitcase as it got stuck on a pebble and moved toward the group with a dogged smile on her face.

Her gaze skipped over the anonymous

faces in an attempt to lock onto the one she knew best, but there was still no sign of him.

"Double-check the knots, Joe," she heard Evan say as he motioned to the slim man who had turned his attention to the rigging on the larger raft that would be used to haul the camp supplies from each location. "I don't mind eating canned beans every night but I'm not sure how well that'll go over with the clients if all our food ends up in the mighty Colorado." Good-natured ribbing and light-hearted laughter followed while Natalie waited for Dan.

She spied a large gnarled piece of wood and, although it didn't look like the most comfortable place to put her rear, at least it wasn't the ground. Out of habit, she glanced at her wrist but her watch was tucked away in her luggage and only a tan line met her eye. Perhaps if Dan didn't show soon, she could ask one of the crew people to radio headquarters or base camp or whatever it was called to find him.

Without meaning to, she found her gaze seeking out the river guide, Evan. He worked quickly and efficiently to get the expedition ready on time, jerking lines to test their strength and helping his colleagues stow luggage on another bargelike raft.

Total eye candy. A dead ringer for Matthew McConaughey if she ever saw one. A candidate for a pinup calendar entitled, "Beach Bum Bachelors." The corners of her lips lifted in amusement as more alliterative calendar names came to mind. Names such as "Randy River Rogues" and "Cute Catches of the Colorado."

When she realized she was staring a bit too intently she tried focusing on something a little less masculine. Besides, as good-looking as he was, he didn't hold a candle to Dan. Of course, she'd never been much for blondes, especially ones with hair that looked perpetually mussed, with the tips bleached white from the sun. It was too bohemian for her tastes. No, she preferred a man with hair as dark and rich as a walnut.

Joe said something just out of Natalie's auditory range and Evan sent a surreptitious glance her way before offering Joe a chuckle.

She stiffened and pretended she didn't notice, then looked out toward the water, entranced by its swift, running surface, until a smiling crew member came to stow her luggage for her.

Feeling oddly vulnerable without something familiar around, she tried shifting to a more comfortable position, but there was no changing the fact her tush was sitting precariously on petrified wood. She didn't have long to move around before Evan started addressing the group and she hurried over to listen.

"Welcome to Wild River Expeditions," he began, rubbing his hands together, his obvious excitement rivaling those of his rafters as they crowded around, eager smiles wreathing their faces. "My name is Evan Murphy and I'll be your guide on this trip." He pointed toward the crew members who were putting the rest of the rafters' luggage on the other rig. "We are here to make your river-rafting experience fun, exciting, something to remember but, more importantly, safe.

"The most valuable skill you can possess to make this trip enjoyable is the ability to listen. The river is a beautiful place but it can be dangerous. You must listen and do as I tell you without hesitation in order to stay safe when we're out there. Together, we'll work as a team to make this the best damn adventure you're ever going to have."

Murmurs of excited agreement rippled

through the small group, but Natalie was too busy watching for another bus and hoping her former fiancé was on it. She frowned when nothing but some indeterminate bird hopped across the path and then flew away. Where was he? Dan was missing all the important stuff. A sliver of irritation followed as her gaze automatically swept the area, again looking for his familiar face.

"Any questions?"

Perhaps he missed his flight or his layover was longer than expected. She sent a worried glance in the direction the bus had gone but there was nothing but scenic nature, pretty as a postcard, staring back.

The hairs rose on the back of her neck and she turned, somehow knowing Evan was staring right at her.

"Any questions?" he asked, his forehead wrinkling in displeasure as if to send home the point that she wasn't listening to the very important things Dan was missing.

"Sorry," she murmured, flushing with embarrassment when the other rafters turned to see who Evan was addressing, knowing she deserved their censure for not paying attention. Panic was beginning to set in and all she could think about was that they were missing the most crucial member of the group.

"All right then, let's get this show on the road!" Evan said, his enthusiasm returning. "You're going to want to change into your swimsuits if you haven't already and grab your hats so we can hop into the boat for some basic instruction before we shove off."

She couldn't let Evan start the trip without Dan. Winding her way through the group as they dispersed to change, Natalie went to tug on Evan's shirt sleeve to catch his attention, but her fingers grazed sun-kissed bare skin instead.

"Oh!" She jerked her hand away as completely inappropriate images of him posing in her fictitious calendar forced their way into her brain. Appalled at herself, she managed to stammer some kind of apology before continuing nervously. "Uh, we can't leave yet. We're missing someone," she said, gesturing desperately at the clipboard in his hand. "Dan Gorlan. He was supposed to be here. Please check your list."

"Gorlan…that name rings a bell." Evan scanned the paperwork, flipping the pages as he searched, and she breathed against the knot in her chest.

Everything was going to be fine. He'd see Dan was missing and he'd send someone to go find him. She'd almost calmed to an acceptable level until he nodded his head, pointing at two names. "Ah, that's right," he said. "I knew I recognized the name. Here it is. Dan Gorlan and Jessica Chambers—canceled. Are they friends of yours?"

Canceled? She wanted to wail at the cosmic cruelty, but she was too stunned by the second bit of information to do more than stare dumbly, her jaw falling slack and her knees wobbling dangerously. "Who's Jessica?" she asked in a guttural whisper.

"I don't know. Maybe one of them got sick. Happens all the time," Evan answered, shifting uncomfortably.

The tears she'd sworn were finished rushed to prove her wrong. He wasn't coming. And even if he had…he'd planned to bring someone else.

"They canceled a few weeks ago," Evan continued awkwardly when she failed to stop staring at him as if he was somehow in on her complete humiliation. "In fact, you and Mrs. Stemming—" he pointed discreetly toward the middle-aged woman wearing an electric blue hat and fussing with her river shoes "—took their places. Otherwise we wouldn't have been able to accommodate your reservations."

Lucky me.

Mortified, Natalie backed away, stumbling on her words as the need to escape swamped her ability to form a coherent sentence.

If she hadn't been choking on a golf-ball-sized clot of misery she would have laughed at the irony. She came all this way for nothing. She blew half her savings on a trip to prove herself to a group of strangers.

And Dan couldn't care less.

The next thing she knew she was moving away, intent on one thing—getting the hell out of there.

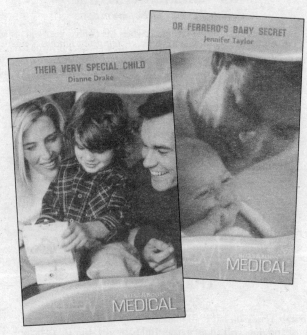

MILLS & BOON®
MEDICAL™
proudly presents

Brides of Penhally Bay

Featuring Dr Nick Tremayne

A pulse-raising collection of emotional, tempting romances and heart-warming stories — devoted doctors, single fathers, Mediterranean heroes, a sheikh and his guarded heart, royal scandals and miracle babies…

Book Five

THE DOCTOR'S ROYAL LOVE-CHILD
by Kate Hardy

on sale 4th April 2008

0208/46/MB132

MILLS & BOON®
INTRIGUE
proudly presents:

Nocturne

A sensual tapestry of spine-tingling passion with heroes and heroines guaranteed to be out of the ordinary

Coming in February 2008 starting with

The Raintree Trilogy

As an ancient foe rises once more, the rejoined battle will measure the endurance of the Raintree clan...

Raintree: Inferno by Linda Howard – **on sale February 2008**
Raintree: Haunted by Linda Winstead Jones – **on sale March 2008**
Raintree: Sanctuary by Beverly Barton – **on sale April 2008**

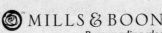

Celebrate 100 years of pure reading pleasure with Mills & Boon®

To mark our centenary, each month we're publishing a special 100th Birthday Edition. These celebratory editions are packed with extra features and include a FREE bonus story.

Plus, starting in February you'll have the chance to enter a fabulous monthly prize draw. See 100th Birthday Edition books for details.

Now that's worth celebrating!

15th February 2008

Raintree: Inferno by Linda Howard
Includes FREE bonus story Loving Evangeline
A double dose of Linda Howard's heady mix of passion and adventure

4th April 2008

The Guardian's Forbidden Mistress by Miranda Lee
Includes FREE bonus story The Magnate's Mistress
Two glamorous and sensual reads from favourite author Miranda Lee!

2nd May 2008

The Last Rake in London by Nicola Cornick
Includes FREE bonus story The Notorious Lord
Lose yourself in two tales of high society and rakish seduction!

Look for Mills & Boon 100th Birthday Editions at your favourite bookseller or visit
www.millsandboon.co.uk

0108/CENTENARY_2-IN-1

2 FREE

BOOKS AND A SURPRISE GIFT!

We would like to take this opportunity to thank you for reading this Mills & Boon® book by offering you the chance to take TWO more specially selected titles from the Superromance series absolutely FREE! We're also making this offer to introduce you to the benefits of the Mills & Boon® Reader Service™—

- ★ **FREE home delivery**
- ★ **FREE gifts and competitions**
- ★ **FREE monthly Newsletter**
- ★ **Exclusive Reader Service offers**
- ★ **Books available before they're in the shops**

Accepting these FREE books and gift places you under no obligation to buy, you may cancel at any time, even after receiving your free shipment. Simply complete your details below and return the entire page to the address below. You don't even need a stamp!

YES! Please send me 2 free Superromance books and a surprise gift. I understand that unless you hear from me, I will receive 4 superb new titles every month for just £3.69 each, postage and packing free. I am under no obligation to purchase any books and may cancel my subscription at any time. The free books and gift will be mine to keep in any case.

U8ZED

Ms/Mrs/Miss/Mr ....Initials ....

BLOCK CAPITALS PLEASE

Surname ....

Address ....

....

....Postcode....................................

Send this whole page to:
UK: FREEPOST CN8I, Croydon, CR9 3WZ

Offer valid in UK only and is not available to current Mills & Boon® Reader Service™ subscribers to this series. Overseas and Eire please write for details and readers in Southern Africa write to Box 3010. Pinegowie. 2123 RSA. We reserve the right to refuse an application and applicants must be aged 18 years or over. Only one application per household. Terms and prices subject to change without notice. Offer expires 30th June 2008. As a result of this application, you may receive offers from Harlequin Mills & Boon and other carefully selected companies. If you would prefer not to share in this opportunity please write to The Data Manager, PO Box 676. Richmond. TW9 IWU.

Mills & Boon® is a registered trademark owned by Harlequin Mills & Boon Limited.
The Mills & Boon® Reader Service™ is being used as a trademark.